PRAISE F...

THE
DECAG...
HOUSE
MURDERS

T0022148

'Fiendish foul play... This is a homage to Golden Age detective fiction, but it's also unabashed entertainment'

SARAH WEINMAN, *NEW YORK TIMES*

'Highly ingenious'

GUARDIAN, BEST CRIME AND THRILLERS

'Very clever indeed'

ANTHONY HOROWITZ

'A terrific mystery, a classic... Very much in the manner of Agatha Christie or John Dickson Carr'

WASHINGTON POST

'A brilliant and richly atmospheric puzzle... Every word counts, leading up to a jaw-dropping but logical reveal'

PUBLISHERS WEEKLY, STARRED REVIEW

'One of the most enjoyable classic crime novels I've ever read. An evocative island setting, a perfectly constructed puzzle, and an entirely satisfying solution. It'll keep you guessing until the very end'

ALEX PAVESI, AUTHOR OF *EIGHT DETECTIVES*

'Behold, the perfect escapist drug! If I could crush this book into a powder and snort it, I would'

VULTURE

'A stunner of a plot, with an ending which I simply could not believe when it was first revealed'

AT THE SCENE OF THE CRIME

'Exceptional... Superbly plotted and wickedly entertaining'

NB MAGAZINE

'A captivating read, culminating in an ending as satisfying as it is shocking... Can stand shoulder to shoulder with the very best mystery novels'

THE JAPAN SOCIETY REVIEW

YUKITO AYATSUJI (born 1960) is a Japanese writer of mystery and horror novels and one of the founding members of the Honkaku Mystery Writers Club of Japan, dedicated to the writing of fair-play mysteries inspired by the Golden Age greats. He started writing as a member of the Kyoto University Mystery Club, which has nurtured many of Japan's greatest crime writers. *The Decagon House Murders* is also available from Pushkin Vertigo.

HO-LING WONG is a translator currently living in the Netherlands. He is also both a member of the Honkaku Mystery Writers Club of Japan and former member of the Kyoto University Mystery Club. He did not commit any murders on Mystery Club excursions.

THE MILL HOUSE MURDERS

YUKITO AYATSUJI

TRANSLATED FROM THE
JAPANESE BY HO-LING WONG

PUSHKIN VERTIGO

Pushkin Press
Somerset House, Strand
London WC2R 1LA

First published by Pushkin Press in 2023

3 5 7 9 8 6 4 2

ISBN 13: 978-1-78227-833-7

Designed and typeset by Tetragon, London
Printed and bound by Clays Ltd, Elcograf S.p.A.

www.pushkinpress.com

To my dear F.S.P.

CONTENTS

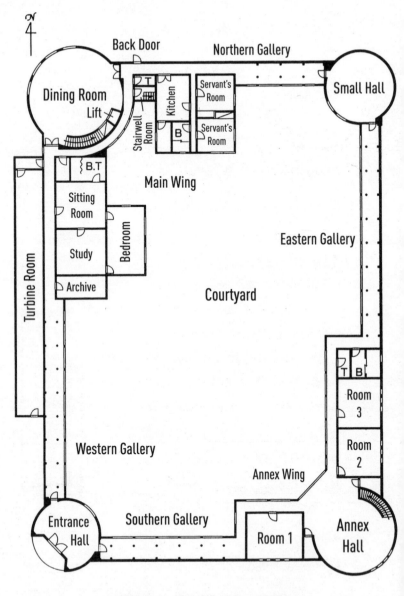

DIAGRAM 1   Mill House Ground Floor

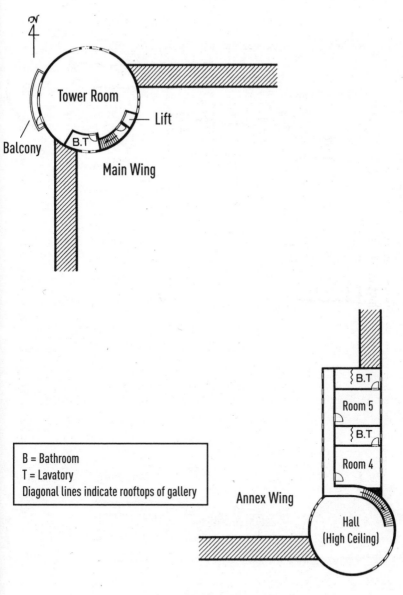

DIAGRAM 2   Mill House First Floor

LIST OF CHARACTERS
(AGES IN SEPTEMBER 1985)

All names in the text of this work are given in Japanese order, family name preceding given name.

Fujinuma Issei	Deceased. A prodigious visionary painter.
Fujinuma Kiichi (41)	Issei's son. Wears a mask to hide his scarred face. Lives in the Mill House.
Fujinuma Yurie (19)	Kiichi's wife. Daughter of Issei's deceased disciple Shibagaki Kōichirō.
Masaki Shingo (38)	Kiichi's friend. Once a disciple of Issei.
Kuramoto Shōji (56)	Butler at the Mill House.
Negishi Fumie (45)	Live-in housekeeper (past).
Nozawa Tomoko (31)	Live-out housekeeper (present).
Ōishi Genzō (49)	Visits the Mill House once a year. Art dealer.
Mori Shigehiko (46)	Visits the Mill House once a year. Professor of art history at M— University.
Mitamura Noriyuki (36)	Visits the Mill House once a year. Director of a surgical hospital.
Furukawa Tsunehito (37)	Visits the Mill House once a year. Deputy priest of the Fujinuma family temple.
Shimada Kiyoshi (36)	An uninvited guest.

PROLOGUE (1985 – 29th September)

The stormy night would soon give way to dawn. A thick bank of clouds slowly parted. Mountain tops covered in a pale mist pierced the eastern sky. While the rumbling of thunder and the heavy rain had passed, the fierce wind showed no sign of relenting. The trees in the forest still creaked as they swayed in the wind, the river was high and the three massive mill wheels kept on turning next to the manor hidden deep in the valley.

It had been a long night, one accompanied by the frantic symphony of the rain, wind, thunder, the raging water in the canal and the mill wheels.

But it was not daybreak that brought them such anxiety. The events of the night had already been enough to feed their fear.

A woman fallen from the tower.

A painting disappeared.

A man vanished under seemingly impossible circumstances.

Could anyone tell where they were heading, where all these events pointed?

The night was drawing to a close. A night that had toyed with them. It was only at dawn that finally, the bizarre culmination of all that had happened in the house would become apparent.

The tower was located in the north-west corner of the mansion. in the section of the hallway that circled in an arc south around the ground floor of the tower, there were two black doors near the eastern end. One was open now. It led into the stairwell, where a narrow flight of stairs spiralled down to the basement. At the bottom of the stairs was a large, bleak room. The lantern-like lamps flickered weakly on the bare concrete walls. A washing machine, dryer and a basket full of clothes stood against the wall near the bottom of the stairs. Several ducts crawled along the ceiling.

Six people were gathered at the back of this gloomy room. Five men, and one woman.

One of the men was seated in a wheelchair. A beautiful girl in a snow-white silk negligee stood close behind him. Two men stood on either side of her, as if to protect her. The other two men stood slightly behind this quartet. All the men were in their pyjamas with some clothes thrown on top.

"Could one of you…" the man in the wheelchair said in a hoarse voice. He was wearing a brown nightshirt, too large for his slim frame, and while it was still only September, he was wearing white gloves. He interlaced his hands on his stomach. "Could one of you open that incinerator door?" He pointed to the incinerator on the other side of the room.

A slight tremor could be heard in his voice. It was probably the tension. However, the man's face was emotionless. This was because he wore a white rubber mask.

One of the men next to the girl stepped forward. He was middle-aged with a ruddy face and a large protruding stomach.

He went over to the incinerator and picked up a black bar lying on the floor. A steel poker.

"Aaah!"

He let out a muffled cry just as he threw the poker away and fell backwards onto the floor.

"What is it, Ōishi?" the masked man in the wheelchair asked.

"It… it's…"

The man with the ruddy face was sitting on the floor, pointing towards where he had dropped the poker.

The girl let out a shriek. The man in the wheelchair turned around to her.

"Yurie, don't look."

"Come on," said the other man who'd been standing by her side as he put his arm around her shoulder and turned her away. He was handsome and tall; the opposite of the man with the ruddy face.

The girl nodded weakly, a terrified look on her face, and walked unsteadily back towards the stairs. The two men who had stood behind—a small man with black-rimmed spectacles and a gloomy-looking larger man—moved in front of the girl, forming a wall to block her view.

Once he was safely out of the girl's sight, the handsome man swiftly walked over to the man with the ruddy face still sitting on the floor, and looked down at him.

"What is it, Mitamura?" the man in the wheelchair asked.

"It's exactly what it looks like, sir," the handsome man replied calmly. "A human finger. Looks like the middle or ring finger."

The man addressed as "sir" pushed his wheelchair over to look for himself. It was ghastly pale, like a dead caterpillar. At one end was an ugly stump covered in dried blood.

"The cut appears to be quite fresh. This finger was probably cut off less than two hours ago," the handsome man said.

"But… what…?"

"That's the question."

The handsome man crouched to get a closer look at the finger lying on the floor.

"Aha… there's a pretty deep indentation here. A mark left by a ring."

"Ah."

The man in the wheelchair put his fingers through the eyeholes of the white mask on his face, placing them on his closed eyelids.

"It has to be Masaki's."

"I'm afraid I must agree," the handsome man replied, standing up once more. The fingers on his right hand started playing with the gold ring on his left ring finger. "I assume it's the mark left by Masaki's cat's eye ring…"

"So he must have murdered Masaki…"

"That I can't say at the moment."

The helpless man with the ruddy face finally managed to get up from the floor.

"Mr Fujinuma, does this mean that inside the incinerator…" he asked, but the man in the wheelchair shook his head ambiguously.

"Could you open the door?"

"But… err…"

The man's cheeks trembled and he looked like he was about to fall over again. The handsome man shrugged and picked up the poker instead.

"I'll do it," he declared as he stepped towards the incinerator. It was a medium-sized incinerator for household garbage, a tarnished silver in colour, set on a concrete base. There was a chimney pipe at the top, right at his eye level, going straight up to the ceiling of the basement room where it disappeared and led outside.

They could hear the crackling of a low fire from inside the metal container. No one, of course, would be burning waste this early in the morning. So why was it lit?

The poker in the handsome man's hand approached the hot door. A metallic clank echoed through the room as he hooked the end of the poker through the handle.

The door swung open. The fire was blazing red inside.

"Uugh."

Everyone covered their noses as a sharp, pungent smell wafted out of the incinerator. A few gagged.

It was the smell of burning meat. But what made the smell especially horrifying was that they all knew what was really burning.

"Masaki…" the man in the wheelchair called out mournfully. "I can't believe this…"

The handsome man stuck the poker in the incinerator. Several blackened objects lay in the fire on top of each other.

He searched the incinerator. He seemed calm, except for the fact that the hand holding the poker was shaking slightly. Eventually he stuck the poker into one of the burning objects and tried to pull it out.

"Waaah!"

He jumped back. As he was pulling the object out, he had inadvertently brought something else with it, which fell onto the floor.

Several loud cries reverberated around the basement.

The handsome man let out a desolate wail as he stared at the round object that was now lying on the floor.

"How horrible…" he whispered.

It was a decapitated human head, burnt black and still smoking. All the hair had been burnt off and the eyes, nose and lips rendered unrecognizable by the blazing heat.

The poker in the man's hand was still sticking into the other burnt object.

"This must be an arm then," he whispered as he threw it into an empty metal bucket nearby, eager to be done with it.

It was indeed an arm.

Like the head on the floor, the arm had been blackened and contorted by the heat. It appeared to be a left arm. But what

17

attracted their attention was the hand: it was missing one finger. The fourth finger counting from the thumb: the left ring finger.

This was the burnt, dead body of a human being.

One body, which had been cut up in six parts, not counting the finger: head, torso, two arms and two legs.

It all happened on a stormy night. And then, finally, dawn arrived.

The shape of the "incidents" inside the house that night had been made clear to everyone present.

The unfortunate woman who fell from the tower. The stolen painting. The suspicious man who disappeared. And in his attempt to catch the thief, another man was killed, cut up in pieces and burnt in the incinerator.

Eventually, the storm passed.

And with that, all the incidents of the night would be buried, hidden away behind one unified explanation.

1 PRESENT (1986 – 28th September)

FUJINUMA KIICHI'S BEDROOM (8:30 A.M.)

I woke as I usually do. The amber curtains were drawn over the windows facing the courtyard to the east, but the bright morning sun shone right through them into the room. It was quiet outside, but if I listened carefully, I could just make out the faint chirping of the mountain birds, as well as the distant sound of flowing water. I could also hear the heavy rumble of the mill wheels, always revolving by the western side of this house. It was a peaceful morning.

We'd had good weather ever since September came along, but the news last night had reported an approaching typhoon. The forecast said it would start raining in the Chūgoku region this afternoon. This morning was thus, truly, the calm before the storm.

I slowly sat up in the spacious bed. The clock on the wall showed half past eight. The same time I always woke up.

Leaning back against the headboard, I reached for the nightstand with my right hand, picked up my old briar pipe and packed it with tobacco. Soon a mellow scent filled the room, accompanied by cream-coloured smoke.

"A typhoon, eh?" I mumbled out loud to myself. My voice was unnaturally hoarse.

I had to think back to exactly one year ago, 28th September. The morning of that fateful day had been the same as today.

There'd been reports of an approaching typhoon then too. And it arrived just as forecast.

One year… A whole year had passed since that blood-soaked night.

I became lost in thought, my hand swaying with the pipe. The tentacles of my mind crept towards the events of that night one year ago, to everything that occurred the following day, and even to what happened afterwards.

I stole a glance at the door in the corner of the room, the bronze doorknob and dark mahogany panelling. That door, which led to the study, would never be opened again…

My lean body suddenly shuddered. An indescribable, inescapable shiver welled up from deep within and ran through my whole being.

It was a quarter to nine now. The phone on my nightstand would ring soon, softly signalling the start of another day.

"Good morning, sir."

The familiar voice on the other end of the line sounded calm. It was the butler, Kuramoto Shōji.

"I will be bringing you your breakfast right away."

"Thanks."

I placed my pipe on its stand and started getting dressed. I took my pyjamas off, put on a shirt and trousers, and a dressing gown on top. When I had managed to do all of this, I put the cotton gloves on both my hands. And finally, it was time to put on my face.

My mask.

That mask was a symbol of my whole life at this time, a symbol of everything that Fujinuma Kiichi now was.

A mask. Indeed, I had no face. I wore that mask every single day to hide my accursed features. The white mask was now the real face of the master of the house. The rubber clung to my skin. A cold death mask worn by a living man.

It was five to nine.

There was a light knock on the door to my right—the door in the corner opposite the study door. This door connected my bedroom to the adjoining sitting room. She—Yurie—had arrived with the usual lovely smile on her face, to bring salvation to my lonely, numb heart.

"Good morning."

Yurie had opened the door with the spare key I had given her. She wore a blinding white dress.

"Have some coffee."

A clear voice came from between her small full lips. I got out of my bed and moved into my wheelchair.

Yurie looked at me silently as she pushed the serving trolley towards me and poured a cup of coffee. I reached for it, looking back at her with my expressionless white mask.

"It's been a whole year," I mumbled, and awaited her reply. But she didn't say anything, so I thanked her for the coffee and took the cup.

A year. On the surface, it seemed time had passed uneventfully. This place deep in the mountains was always tranquil, almost as if time itself had forgotten about us here. The fresh water flowing through the valley never stopped turning the three mill wheels of the house. Yurie, Kuramoto and myself lived peacefully here. Save for the housekeeper, we had no visitors.

Nothing had changed. At least, nothing appeared to have changed. However, I knew this house had undergone a great transformation. It was, of course, all because of what happened last year.

A man and a woman had died, and another man disappeared…

Those events must have had a tremendous impact on the mind of Yurie, this young girl. Perhaps the scars would never heal. I had also changed.

I squinted beneath my mask and watched Yurie as I silently brought the cup to my mouth. Yurie. The only woman I had ever loved. A beautiful girl who had spent her teenage years in solitude in the tower room of this house.

Yurie was slim and 150 centimetres tall. She was rather fair for a Japanese person, with firm smooth skin. Her luscious hair hung down to her waist.

Yes, she too had changed. The faraway look I was used to seeing in her eyes had altered subtly. She had started to prepare coffee all by herself in the morning and bring it to me in my room. Sometimes she would go outside to enjoy the running water or the beauty of the garden. She had also learned to show her own emotions more openly—to some extent.

She had changed in many ways. But how was I to welcome such a transformation?

"You look lovely this morning too. You are becoming more beautiful with each passing day."

She blushed and averted her eyes.

"They will be arriving in the afternoon. I hope you're not scared," I told her.

After a moment's silence, Yurie softly laid her hand on my shoulder. The scent of coffee and tobacco was joined by a sweet fragrance.

"I'm a little bit afraid," she replied. "But I think I'll be fine."

"There's nothing to be afraid of," I said with the gentlest voice I could muster. "Everything is over now. Nothing will happen this year."

But was that really so? Would nothing really happen this year?

I shook my head determinedly at the question. Nothing would happen. Nothing at all. Not unless the man who disappeared that night should appear, roaming this house like a spectre.

For a moment Yurie and I looked at each other in silence. She was unable to hide a shadow of fear that passed over her face.

"Please, play the piano for me later."

She nodded lightly and smiled at me.

DINING ROOM (9:30 A.M.)

"Is everything ready for today?"

I was sitting in the dining room on the ground floor of the tower. It was a spacious round hall, with a ceiling two storeys high. I had posed the question to Kuramoto Shōji after finishing my breakfast with Yurie at the round table.

Kuramoto, dressed in a dark-grey three-piece suit, was busy pouring another cup of coffee for Yurie. He quickly answered in the affirmative and with the serving tray in his hand, he turned carefully to me.

"All three guest rooms on the ground floor of the annex are ready. The guests are scheduled to arrive at two o'clock. Tea will be served in the annex hall at three, dinner here at half past six. The schedule is the same as previous years. I hope these arrangements are to your liking?"

"I'll leave it all up to you."

"Understood."

You could safely call Kuramoto a large man. He was tall with strong, broad shoulders. There were some grey streaks in his swept-back hair. His jaw was wide and square and his eyes were small as grains of rice. He was in his mid-fifties. A smile never appeared on his pale, wrinkly face no matter what happened. His loud baritone voice was just as cold as his face, if not even colder.

But that was exactly why the title of butler, almost extinct in modern-day Japan, suited him. Silently managing the house with the one goal of serving his master. Able to do his work without letting his feelings interfere. One could call it a talent—if so, Kuramoto was a natural.

The butler, still standing straight as an arrow, opened his mouth once more.

"After you retired to your room last night, you received a telephone call."

"A call for me?"

"Yes. But they said there was no need to speak to you directly, so they stated their business to me."

"And?"

Kuramoto was silent for a moment.

"It was a phone call from Mr Nīmura of the police."

Nīmura was a chief inspector of the First Investigation Division of the Okayama Prefectural Police Department. He had headed the investigation into the incidents a year ago.

"He told me that someone might be coming here today."

I cocked my head in curiosity as I waited for Kuramoto's further explanation.

"Apparently he's coming from Kyūshū, the younger brother of an acquaintance of Mr Nīmura in the Ōita Prefectural Police Department. Mr Nīmura said he was a rather odd man."

"And why would he be coming here?"

"Apparently he's interested in what happened last year. He visited Mr Nīmura out of the blue, asking him about the incidents, and then asked to know our exact location, mumbling something about coming today. Mr Nīmura sounded terribly sorry. He explained that he wasn't able to send him away, considering he was the brother of an acquaintance."

I lighted my pipe as I asked: "Hm. And his name?"

"The man's name is Shimada."

Not a name I knew. And I had no intention of welcoming an unknown visitor. Why else would I be living in this secluded place, in the mountains far away from town, wearing a mask to cover my face?

"What should I do?" Kuramoto asked.

"Send him away."

"Understood."

Neither Yurie nor I wanted to think about the incidents ever again. The two of us had worked desperately this year to eliminate the memories of that night, memories that threatened our peaceful lives. It was out of the question to have someone prying into our business.

But even without this Shimada, I was afraid that on this particular day I should be prepared for the memories to come back anyway.

28th September. Ōishi Genzō, Mori Shigehiko, Mitamura Noriyuki. The day of the three visitors.

HALLWAY   (9:55 A.M.)

We left the dining room by the south doors. Yurie pushed my wheelchair.

"Would you like to go back to your room?"

I shook my head and told her I wanted to go around the galleries.

The spacious courtyard, maintained in a traditional Japanese garden style, was on the other side of the row of hallway windows.

We would keep the garden to our right as we slowly walked around the tower.

Sunlight danced on the grey carpet. The water in the oval pond at the centre of the courtyard shone brightly. There was a path covered by white gravel, and faded shrubs here and there.

At the end of the semi-circular row of windows was a black door on the right, and behind it was the staircase leading to the basement.

I couldn't help but avert my eyes, afraid the door would bring up memories of that terrible night. Yurie did the same.

But the door suddenly opened from the other side. I was frozen in shock.

"Oh, good morning."

A slender woman in her thirties appeared from the stairwell. It was the day housekeeper, Nozawa Tomoko.

She had replaced our previous housekeeper at the end of last year. She usually came three times a week from town, but I had asked her to stay at the house these three days, from yesterday through tomorrow.

She was wearing an apron and holding a large laundry basket. She turned her face slightly away from me and stood still, waiting for us to pass by.

Tomoko was a silent, gloomy woman. She was the exact opposite of the live-in housekeeper who used to work here, Negishi Fumie.

Tomoko was similar to Kuramoto in the sense that she would quietly do whatever job she was tasked with, but I didn't like her timid personality. And like Kuramoto, I could not read what was really on her mind, something that at times would irritate me greatly.

For example, what did she think of the married couple with such an age gap between them living in this odd house?

"Err, sir…"

It was rare for her to address me without being spoken to first.
"Yes?"

"About the basement room…"

"What about it?" I asked.

"I've been thinking for a while about whether I should bring it up. But I can't help it, it's eerie…"

Her feeling was only natural. Anyone who knew about the incidents last year would feel the same. I stopped her with a raised hand.

"The incinerator has been replaced. I also had the place thoroughly cleaned," I explained.

"Ah, yes, I am aware of that. But still… And there's this smell sometimes…"

"Smell?" I repeated.

"Yes, an unpleasant smell…"

"Surely it's your imagination."

"Well, perhaps, but…"

"Enough." I bluntly cut her off when I heard a whimper of fright escaping from Yurie's mouth. "You can consult Kuramoto about it."

"Yes, I'm sorry."

We watched Tomoko as she practically fled the scene and then I turned to Yurie.

"Don't mind her."

She nodded gently and started pushing my wheelchair again.

We turned right at the end of the hallway and continued towards the north-east corner of the house, with the northern outer wall of the building on our left. This section of the house was called the Northern Gallery.

Beyond the kitchen and the servants' quarters, the Northern Gallery became almost twice as wide, expanding to the right in the direction of the courtyard. It continued in a straight line to the door at the far end. A grey carpet covered the floor of the gallery, but the wider section had a parquet floor. Windows were installed in the right wall at regular intervals, affording a view of the courtyard.

Oil paintings of various sizes hung on the left wall of the gallery. They were fantastical landscapes, as seen through the mind's eye of the prodigious painter Fujinuma Issei.

Those three men would come here today once again. Their goal was to look at these paintings—but they probably also wanted to get their hands on them.

This house welcomes guests only once a year. Only today, on 28th September, the day Fujinuma Issei passed away.

Today is also the day that the housekeeper, Negishi Fumie, met her tragic end. And tomorrow, 29th September, yes, is the day Masaki Shingo, the man who was once Fujinuma Issei's disciple, departed this world.

"Perhaps I should have Kuramoto arrange some flowers," I suddenly said out loud.

"Flowers?" Yurie cocked her head. My comment had surprised her. "Why?"

"To mourn the dead," I said in a low voice. "In particular to mourn his… to mourn Masaki Shingo's death."

"Please don't talk about it any more."

Yurie looked at my masked face. Her black eyes, clear as glass, started to tear up.

"It breaks my heart…"

"Breaks your heart, you say?"

My lips formed a wry smile as my mind was swept away, back to the events of exactly one year ago.

FUJINUMA KIICHI'S BEDROOM   (8:30 A.M.)

He woke as he usually did. The amber curtains were drawn over the windows facing the courtyard to the east, but the bright morning sun shone right through them into the room. It was quiet outside, but if he listened carefully, he could just make out the faint chirping of the mountain birds, as well as the distant sound of flowing water. He could also hear the heavy rumble of the mill wheels, always revolving by the western side of the house. It was a peaceful morning.

The news last night had reported an approaching typhoon. The forecast said it would start raining in the Chūgoku region on the afternoon of the 28th.

He slowly sat up in the spacious bed. The clock on the wall showed half past eight. The same time he always woke up.

Leaning back against the headboard, he reached for the night-stand with his right hand, picked up his old briar pipe and packed it with tobacco. Soon a mellow scent filled the room, accompanied by cream-coloured smoke.

Three days ago he'd caught a cold and ran a fever, but he'd recovered now. He could savour the scent of tobacco again.

He slowly closed his eyes as he puffed his pipe.

28th September. Ōishi Genzō, Mori Shigehiko, Mitamura Noriyuki and Furukawa Tsunehito. Today was the day the four of them would visit him in the afternoon, just as they had done in previous years.

Their annual visit was not a joyous occasion for him, living as he did in this house deep in the mountains, hiding from the outside world. He honestly felt their visit was a great annoyance.

Yet he was also in denial about his feelings. He could easily tell them not to come if he genuinely did not want them to. But his inability to turn them away all these years was perhaps partially due to guilt.

He kept his eyes closed as a low sigh escaped his cracked lips.

Anyway, they're coming today. It'd all been decided, so nothing could be changed now.

He had no intention of making a detailed analysis of his own contradictory thoughts. The visit plagued him, but he also welcomed it. That was all there was to it.

It was a quarter to nine now. The phone on his nightstand would ring soon, softly signifying the start of another day.

"Good morning, sir."

The familiar voice on the other end of the line sounded calm. It was the butler, Kuramoto Shōji.

"How are you feeling, sir?"

"Better now, thanks."

"I can bring your breakfast immediately if you wish."

"I'll come down myself."

He placed his pipe on its stand and started getting dressed. He took his pyjamas off, put on a shirt and trousers, and a dressing gown on top. When he had managed to do all of this, he put the cotton gloves on both his hands. And finally, it was time to put on his face.

His mask.

The mask could be considered the symbol of the last twelve years of his life, a symbol of everything that Fujinuma Kiichi was.

Indeed, he had no face. He wore this mask every single day to hide his accursed features. This white mask bearing the features of Fujinuma Kiichi, the master of this house. The rubber clung to his skin. A cold death mask worn by a living man.

It was five to nine.

There was a knock on the door connecting his bedroom to the adjoining sitting room.

"Enter," he commanded.

A short, plump woman opened the door with the spare key he had given her. She was wearing a pristine white apron.

"Good morning," said the live-in housekeeper, Negishi Fumie.

"I've brought you your medicine. How are you feeling? Oh, you're dressed already? Will you be wearing a tie today? Oh, dear, smoking the pipe again? It's not good for your health, you know. I'd appreciate it if you'd listen to my advice for once."

Fumie was forty-five, four years older than her master, but still energetic and lively. Big eyes adorned her round face, and she always spoke quickly in a high-pitched voice.

The expressionless masked master stared at her as he ignored her chatter and started to get out of bed. Fumie immediately tried to help, but he stopped her.

"I can do this myself," he said in a hoarse voice. He moved his lean, weak body into the wheelchair.

"Here's your medicine."

"I don't need it any more."

"Oh, no, that won't do. Please take it for one more day to be on the safe side. Especially considering we'll be having visitors. Today will be more taxing for you than usual."

He gave in, took the pills handed over to him and swallowed them together with a glass of water. Fumie looked pleased and nodded as she held the handles of the wheelchair.

"And you'd better not take a bath today yet. Let's see how that fever fares first."

He sighed inwardly. He wished she'd let him be, but it was her former profession as a nurse showing through. When it came to his health, she never stopped.

She was an attentive woman who liked to care for others. A previous marriage had failed, but she didn't seem hurt by the experience. She did everything, from running the house to taking care of him, helping him bathe and cutting his hair, even monitoring his health.

He wouldn't have liked Fumie to be like Kuramoto, a "robot" who always kept an appropriate distance from his master. But he did wish she'd be a bit less talkative.

"Shall I bring you to the dining room now? Oh, no pipe for you any more, leave that thing here. Let's go."

She pushed the wheelchair out of the bedroom.

"The young lady and Masaki are already in the dining room."

"Yurie too?"

"Yes, it's good to see her now. She's much livelier than before. Sir, you know what I think? I think she should get out more often."

"What?"

The face beneath his mask suddenly froze as he turned around to Fumie. She shuddered and fell silent.

"I-I'm sorry."

"Forget it," he said bluntly, and faced frontwards again.

After breakfast Fujinuma Yurie returned alone to her room up in the tower.

She was a beautiful girl who looked as if she had stepped right out of a painting and didn't seem to be made of mere flesh and blood. She had clear black eyes, soft pink lips, smooth fair skin and gorgeous black hair. Her features were delicate and refined.

Yurie was nineteen years old, turning twenty the following spring. Normally, a woman her age wouldn't be called a "girl" any more. But her delicate physique seemed far removed from the ideal of a fully developed woman. Her woeful look, always peering far away into the distance, was heart-wrenching.

A beautiful girl. Yes, that was the only way to describe her.

Dressed in a lemon-coloured blouse, Yurie leaned against the white window frame and stared absent-mindedly at the view outside.

Mountains stretched far into the distance, seeming to overlap each other, while a richly green river snaked through the valleys between them. The peaks of the mountain range pierced the sky and above them dark-grey clouds were slowly gathering.

Soon autumn would take over, changing the colours of the landscape. And then winter would come and the whole world visible from this tower would be painted snow-white. How many such changing seasons had she witnessed from here? Always from this same window, always in this room.

The large circular room was at the top of the tower in the north-west corner of the house. The dining room below had a two-storey high ceiling, so this room was, for all intents and purposes, on the second floor.

The walls were a calm pearl-grey colour and a pale fluffy carpet covered the floor. A large chandelier hung from the centre of the dark-brown panelled ceiling. The windows were so small that it was dark inside the room even though it was morning.

Yurie stepped away from the window and sat down on the canopy bed. Opposite her, on the south side of the room, was a dividing wall, with the doors to the staircase on one side and her own bathroom on the other. Behind a third door, brown metal this time, was the lift for the wheelchair-bound master of the house.

Gorgeous pieces of furniture were scattered about the room with lots of space between them—a wardrobe, dressing table, shelf, sofas and even a grand piano. Several oil paintings adorned the remaining wall surface, all of them by Fujinuma Issei in his characteristic fantastical style.

The girl had lived here for ten years. In this house, in this valley, in this tower room.

Ten years ago, Yurie had been nine, still in the third grade. Her mother had passed away soon after giving birth to her only child. Then in October of 1973, when Yurie was seven, her father Shibagaki Kōichirō had passed away at the young age of thirty-one after an illness. With no other relatives, Yurie was all alone.

She could vaguely remember her father's death. A hospital room with cold, white walls. A bed that smelled of medicine. Her father coughing violently. Blood everywhere, staining the sheets. Adults wearing white uniforms quickly leading her from the room…

The next thing she remembered was crying in someone's warm embrace. She knew the person's face. It was "Uncle Fujinuma", who had often visited their house even before her father fell ill.

34

Not long after, things were arranged so Yurie would be taken in by Fujinuma Kiichi. Knowing he did not have long to live, her father Kōichirō had asked Kiichi for this favour. Fujinuma Kiichi was the only son of the painter Fujinuma Issei, who had been Shibagaki Kōichirō's mentor.

Very soon after Kiichi had taken in Yurie, he was responsible for a car accident, which caused severe damage to his face and limbs. Kiichi left his birthplace of Kōbe and decided to have this curious house built deep in the mountains. Two years later, in 1975, this was where he had brought Yurie.

Yurie had spent the next ten years here, more or less locked inside the house. This house, this room and the view from the windows were the whole world to her. She'd spent her adolescence without school, without friends, without a television or magazines, without any idea of how other young people her age were living their lives under the same sky.

A delightful melody began to escape from between her lips. She got up from her bed and walked towards the piano.

Her slender fingers fell on the keyboard and she started playing to accompany the tune she was humming.

It was Claude Debussy's "La fille aux cheveux de lin", a piece taught to her by Masaki Shingo, the friend of Kiichi's who had come to live in the house six months earlier.

It was a short piece. While she had only barely memorized it, her fingers eventually managed to get to the end. She then walked over to the balcony on the western side of her room.

The air outside was unpleasantly humid. Her hair fluttered in an eerie, warm southern breeze that swept up from the ground. The sound of the water flowing below and the mill wheels turning was louder than usual.

"I'm afraid…" she whispered to herself.

It was perhaps the first time that this girl, who'd been imprisoned for ten years, truly experienced fear.

FRONT GARDEN   (10:10 A.M.)

Three gigantic mill wheels, each well over five metres in diameter,
turned ceaselessly, making a loud, low rumbling noise as their
black blades splashed into the water. Their relentless movement
was reminiscent of a steam locomotive.

Fujinuma Kiichi—his own face hidden by the white rubber
mask—had gone out to the paved front garden to stare at the face
of the house he had chosen as his home. Standing next to him
was a skinny man, dressed in brown trousers and a dark-grey
shirt. His arms were folded and he looked serious.

"Mr Fujinuma, you know what I think those wheels look like?"
He unfolded his arms as he awaited a reaction from Fujinuma
Kiichi, who'd been silent the whole time the two were standing
there.

"Well, what do they look like?" asked the hoarse voice from
beneath the mask.

"They almost look like they are turning against the flow of
time, keeping the house and everything in this valley frozen in
a never-ending moment."

"Hm. Always the poet," the masked man said, looking up at
him. But he then sighed at his words. For who was it who had
put this "poet" on his current path?

The man's name was Masaki Shingo, an old friend of Kiichi's.
Both hailed from the city of Kōbe. Masaki was thirty-eight, three
years younger. They had first become acquainted during their
college years when they joined the same arts club.

36

Kiichi had soon realized that he was not an artistic prodigy like his father Fujinuma Issei. Kiichi had studied economics at a local university, and after graduating used some of his father's money to get started in real estate, where he'd been successful.

Masaki on the other hand had both the talent and the passion to become an artist, but following his parents' wishes, he had chosen to pursue the law. However, one day Fujinuma Issei happened to glimpse one of his works and sang its praises. This had changed Masaki's future. He decided to drop out of university, going against the will of his father, who ran an accountancy firm in his home town. His destiny was to be an artist, and Issei would be his mentor.

"How ironic fate can be," Kiichi thought to himself. The son of a genius painter becomes a businessman, and the son of an accountant becomes a painter... Back when he'd seen Masaki's art, his feelings had been quite complicated. He may not have had the talent to be an artist himself, but he could recognize the true value of a painting. Kiichi had prided himself on this, and in his eyes Masaki's future looked bright indeed. Yurie's father Shibagaki Kōichirō had also been a disciple of Issei around the same time, but the difference in talent between the two was all too obvious to Kiichi.

Masaki's brushstrokes showed unrestrained imagination, and he created unique worlds. His work rivalled even that of his mentor Issei. Yet unlike Issei, whose fantastical paintings were born of his imagination, Masaki's works seemed to be telling the viewer something about reality. In Kiichi's eyes, Masaki was a poet.

But Masaki's and Kiichi's lives had changed forever on that winter day twelve years ago, the day of the accident.

Masaki Shingo had disappeared from Kiichi's life over the last decade, but in April this year, he had suddenly reappeared to ask for Kiichi's help.

He'd pleaded with Kiichi not to ask any questions. He hadn't told Kiichi why, but asked if he could stay in the house for a while.

Kiichi understood right away that Masaki had only asked the favour because he had found himself in a difficult situation. Masaki told Kiichi that his parents had already passed away and that he had nowhere else to go now, but it was obvious something fishy was going on. Kiichi even suspected that Masaki might be on the run from the police, but despite that he welcomed Masaki into his home without any hesitation, though he could have easily refused.

"Fumie told me that Yurie has been more cheerful lately," Kiichi said as he looked up at the tower to his left. "I should thank you for that."

"Me?" Masaki repeated, slightly startled. Kiichi nodded gently.

"Yurie seems quite fond of you."

"I guess rediscovering the piano has helped. She started learning when she was five, right?"

"Yes, but only for a short while, until her father passed away," Kiichi recalled.

"She's got talent. She's mastered the fundamentals already. It's been a pleasure to teach her."

"And I'm grateful for that. But…"

"Mr Fujinuma, I hope you aren't…" Masaki said hesitantly.

"What?"

"I hope you aren't imagining anything…" Masaki touched his thin moustache for a moment, and then chuckled. "Oh, sorry."

"What's so funny?"

"I hope that as Yurie's husband, you don't suspect me of inappropriate behaviour…"

"Of course not."

Kiichi stared at his old friend from beneath his mask. Masaki was a handsome man with finely chiselled features. He hadn't changed a bit over the years. No, that wasn't true. Looking at him now, Kiichi could see that the brilliance he once radiated was gone. The colour of his skin had changed, and the light in his eyes had dimmed.

"There's absolutely nothing to fret about, I assure you," Masaki said.

Kiichi remained silent.

"There's no cause for concern. I simply can't look at her as a woman. The same way you, her husband, can't see her as your wife."

Kiichi could think of no reply. He bit his dry lips in response.

"She's still a child. And perhaps, she'll be one for ever," Masaki said.

"For ever…" Kiichi averted his gaze from his friend. "Yurie has kept barriers around her all this time. Ever since her father died twelve years ago and when we came to live here. For ten years."

"But, that's because…" Masaki interrupted, but Kiichi carried on.

"I know. It's my own fault. It's because I kept her here, confined to the tower. Fearing her mind would turn to the outside world and that she'd leave me."

"Do you regret it?" Masaki asked his friend.

"I'd be lying if I said no."

"I'm not here to pry," Masaki said as he retrieved a crushed cigarette box from his breast pocket. "But I think I know what's on your mind."

Kiichi stayed silent again so he went on.

"I suspect that you admire Yurie in the same way you'd look at the paintings by Master Issei. You wanted to keep her locked up here, on display, together with Fujinuma Issei's beautiful landscapes, right?"

"Yes…" A grunt escaped from Kiichi's throat. "You really are a poet."

"I'm no poet," said Masaki. He shrugged and put a cigarette between his lips. "Even if I used to be one, I stopped twelve years ago."

Masaki pretended not to mind, but it was painfully clear to Kiichi even now how frustrated Masaki must still feel. The accident happened twelve long years ago, but Kiichi still regretted it.

The rumble of the unrelenting water mill brought him back to that day, to that night, to the blast of destruction. The wheels turning on and on, crashing relentlessly…

Fujinuma Kiichi's gloved hands moved to cover his ears.

"The sky doesn't look promising," Masaki said in an attempt to change the subject. He was looking up. "Seems like it'll really start to pour in the afternoon, like the forecast said."

Dark clouds were slowly approaching from beyond the grey stone walls of the tower. A large shadow fell upon the house and its surroundings.

3 PRESENT (1986 – 28th September)

FRONT GARDEN (10:40 A.M.)

The main entrance to the Mill House is located in its south-west corner. A terraced paved garden fans out from the entrance towards the east. Low box hedges separate the individual levels, each about three metres wide. Surrounding the garden is a gloomy forest—a bleak, stark sight.

Yurie pushed my wheelchair down the gentle slope. We crossed the bridge over the canal dug to power the mill wheels, heading towards the western side of the house.

There was a low, reverberating rumble up ahead as we approached the mill wheels. We stared at the black blades churning the water as we passed by, going down another paved slope towards a forest path that ran parallel to the river.

The Mill House lay deep in the mountains in the north of Okayama Prefecture. It was a one-hour drive from the town of A—, where the closest bus stop was. Some people also called our home Mask Manor, after its unusual-looking master.

Yurie and I had developed a habit of gazing at the house's mill wheels turning and listening to their crashing from this spot. As we did so, I'd close my eyes and try to find some inner peace.

The whole forest around us swayed in the wind. Fresh water flowed from the canal in front of us and into the river beyond.

The mill wheels' relentless turning was solely in order to power the house. The valley was trying to keep us here, to stop the flow of time and possess what remained of my and Yurie's lives.

I heard her give a faint sigh, so I turned to look up at her.

"Yurie, what's the matter? Are you ill?"

"No." She shook her head. "I just feel so... lonely."

"Lonely?" It was the first time I had heard her use that word. "Is it because we live here, like this?"

"... I don't know," she said, looking up at the tower to our left. Her face was pale. "I'm sorry, it's silly."

"Not at all," I said to her. But in truth, my feelings on her confession were complicated.

I knew very well that Yurie lived a solitary life. She'd lost her parents at a young age, and for more than a decade since then she had lived in this house, without a single friend. She hadn't gone to school. She had barely been to town. There were restrictions on what she could read. She hadn't even ever watched any television until last year.

Whenever I was able to consider the matter in a rational manner, I knew that in the end I had to free her from this isolated place. But was that still possible?

Yurie stared silently at the tower that had imprisoned her for so many years. As I gazed at her profile, I was reminded of her father, Shibagaki Kōichirō.

The man had passion, dedication and more than enough talent, but in the end, he could only ever imitate his mentor Issei's works. The man had died far too young, so his absolute masterpiece was probably his daughter rather than any work of art. It was a cruel thought, to dismiss his art that way, but I couldn't help myself.

The noise of the mill wheels took my thoughts away from Shibagaki Kōichirō's death, and towards the accident on a night two months later. My mind began to turn with the wheels.

It was the night of 24th December 1973. Three people were in the car: Fujinuma Kiichi, Masaki Shingo and Masaki's fiancée, Hotta Keiko. It was a cold Christmas Eve. The engaged couple had been invited to a party at the Fujinuma residence in Kōbe, and were just on their way home.

The wind was blowing hard, and snow was falling. The temperature had plunged that evening and the wet roads had frozen over.

The crash of the mill wheels was drowned out by another noise of destruction.

I covered my ears but when I dropped my hands I could still hear the sound of the running engine. The sound wasn't coming from the past, I realized. It was coming from right behind us.

FRONT GARDEN   (11:00 A.M.)

Yurie turned around and gasped.

"It's a red car."

I turned my wheelchair about too. It was difficult to spot it among the thick, colourful autumn leaves, but eventually I managed to make out a car on the forest path beneath us.

After a while, the noise of the engine stopped. The door on the driver's side opened and a man emerged.

"Ah, so this is the place," he said out loud. He took a few steps up the paved slope, stretched his body and then shaded his eyes with his hand as he looked up at us.

"Mr Fujinuma, I presume?" he asked in the same loud voice.

I did not react. Yurie's hands gripped the handles of my wheel-chair like a frightened child's.

"What an amazing house! Far more impressive than I expected."

The man was tall and thin, almost too thin. He was wearing a pair of black jeans and an ivory button-down. He kept his hands in his pockets while he climbed the slope towards us with long strides.

"The Mill House… Aha, indeed it is."

He stopped next to us and looked up at the three mill wheels.

"Is the front entrance on the other side of that bridge? I see you have stone walls… Hmm, yes, yes. Oh, there's even a tower. You have your own castle with a mill.

"When you hear the word 'mill,' the first thing most people think of is a small, cosy mill like the one from the children's song 'The Mill in the Black Forest'. I'm more inclined to think of the seven mill wheels of Asakura in Fukuoka Prefecture. Can you believe how impressed I was when I first saw them? I was still a child then, and for some reason the wheels scared me. They seemed like gigantic monsters. As if they could suddenly break free and roll towards you… But your three mill wheels here are at least as magnificent. And what an interesting idea to attach them to a Western-style country house. That Nakamura Seiji is really…"

"Did you say Nakamura Seiji?" I repeated.

"Oh, please excuse me for rambling on. Am I correct in assuming you're Fujinuma Kiichi?"

The man looked down at me, a wide smile on his face. This was the first time we'd met, but he didn't seem at all disturbed by my mask.

"You must be Shimada. Is that right?" I asked in my hoarse voice. The man nodded.

"Oh, did that inspector I met yesterday call you? I suppose he felt guilty about me." The man brushed back his light wavy hair as he formally introduced himself. "The name is Shimada Kiyoshi, nice to meet you. I'm terribly sorry for my unannounced visit."

He appeared to be in his mid-thirties, and somehow as if he could be very difficult to deal with depending on the situation.

"Shimada Kiyoshi, eh?" I said as I looked him up and down. "I was told you are interested in the incidents that occurred here last year."

"Well, yes, put simply, that's true," Shimada replied, a slightly tense expression on his face. "But I haven't come here just to gossip. You see, I'm not a disinterested party."

"What do you mean?"

"You know Furukawa Tsunehito, right?" he asked me.

"Furukawa? But he's…"

"The man who disappeared last year. I'm actually a friend of his. You know he was the deputy priest of a Buddhist temple in Takamatsu, right? My family also runs a temple in Kyūshū, and we got to know each other when we were younger. We were both at a university specializing in Buddhist studies. He was in the year above me."

"Ah," I said and nodded as I stole a glance at Yurie. She was looking down at Shimada's legs, still tightly gripping the handles of my wheelchair. It was obvious to me that she was frightened of him. It was a natural reaction, of course. An unknown visitor suddenly appears, and of all people he asks about Furukawa Tsunehito…

"Yurie, go back to the house," I ordered her. "It's all right. I can wheel myself."

"Yes, OK then."

I watched as Yurie walked silently away from us.

"She's your wife, right?" Shimada said, seemingly impressed. "She's much… how should I put it… more beautiful than I imagined."

Apparently he had done his homework. I glared at him again as he ran his hands through his hair.

"I'd heard stories about the Mill House before. I mean, Kōjin told me. And then all of that happened last year, right? I couldn't believe it when I first heard."

Shimada had called Furukawa Tsunehito "Kōjin". For a moment, I wondered where the name had come from, but then I realized it was an alternate way to read the characters used to write the given name "Tsunehito". He probably liked wordplay.

Furukawa Tsunehito. The man who mysteriously disappeared a year ago, on that stormy night. The man believed to have stolen a painting by Fujinuma Issei, killed Masaki Shingo, cut his body into pieces, burned it in the incinerator and to have been on the run ever since.

As Shimada had explained, Furukawa was indeed the son of the head priest of a temple in Takamatsu and worked there as the deputy priest. That temple had also been the Fujinuma family temple for generations.

"Mr Fujinuma, I'd like to ask you honestly… What do you think?"

"About what?"

"Do you think he—Kōjin—is really behind what happened last year?"

"Could it have been anybody else?"

I asked the question rhetorically and shook my head.

"I see." Shimada shrugged and then looked straight at my white mask. "But something about the case bothers me. There's something not right…"

"I assume that's because you're his friend."

"Of course, I'll admit that's part of it. The Kōjin I knew is a timid man, nervous to a fault. I simply can't imagine him committing a murder. But that doesn't sound convincing at all, does it, right? That is just my personal impression of him."

"So?" I couldn't hide my irritation any more and raised my voice. "Why have you come here, on this day? Is there something you have to say to me?"

"Have I offended you?"

"I want to forget about what happened," I explained to him.

"I understand that. I'm aware you are not fond of visitors in general. I'm also familiar with the events that led to you living deep in the mountains, behind a mask."

"Well then…"

"I must apologize." Shimada bowed his head modestly. But then he quickly raised it again. "Nonetheless, I had to come here." He'd spoken these words in a low, grave voice that made his words strangely persuasive. He looked up at the mill once more.

"I believe this house was constructed eleven years ago?"

"Yes, that's right."

"This canal had to be dug especially to get the water from the river here, right? It must have been a tremendous project, and all just for a private residence. Is the power generated by those mill wheels used for something?"

I nodded silently. He looked around and then continued his questions.

"Aha, so that's it. That's a telephone line over there, I think? But I can't see a power line. You generate your own power with these mill wheels?"

"Indeed."

"Ha-ha, how wonderful." Shimada crossed his arms and admired the house with avid interest. After a moment of silence, he muttered to himself: "So this is Nakamura Seiji's Mill House…"

I could barely make out the words. Nakamura Seiji. He had already mentioned the name once before. What did he know about Nakamura Seiji? I couldn't contain myself any longer.

"Why do you mention that name?"

"Oh, did I say that out loud?" He turned back to me. "You see, I have a curious connection with him. After what happened here last year, I started to look into the affair myself the best I could. I was very surprised when I stumbled on the fact that Nakamura Seiji designed this house. It felt almost like… fate."

"Fate?"

"Oh, let's leave it at that for now. I'll tell you about it another time." Shimada pursed his lips and then narrowed his eyes. "By the way, you asked me why I came. To tell you the truth, half the reason is sheer coincidence."

"Coincidence?"

"I didn't drive down here all the way from Kyūshū to prove Kōjin's innocence or to find him or anything like that."

"Oh?"

"I have an old friend who lives in Shizuoka, and I was on my way there. But yesterday, when I drove into this prefecture, I suddenly remembered that today was that fateful day—28th September."

"And you just decided to come here on a whim?"

"Well, I wouldn't call it a whim as such. What happened last year has haunted me ever since, and I've long wanted to take a look at the Mill House, at this creation of Nakamura Seiji, for myself. And then I also have this habit of not being able to stop once I've set my mind to something…"

"Hm."

I placed my gloved hands on the armrests of my wheelchair.

"And what is it you want to do next?" I asked him.

"With your permission, I'd like to join the gathering at your house today, in Kōjin's place. You see, I'm also really interested in the paintings of Fujinuma Issei. I request this favour of you knowing very well how impertinent it is to ask."

"You have my permission."

Was I really going to let this man inside the house? I had to reluctantly squash down the objections that rose inside me. Why had I said yes?

The main reason was his incessant hinting at some connection between himself and the architect, Nakamura Seiji. But that wasn't all. I could feel from the aura he exuded that it would be futile to try and thwart his wishes.

"I'll have a room made ready for you," I said to him. "If you drive up the slope and turn left, you'll find a place to park."

The wind began to pick up and dark clouds gathered in the sky, hiding the sun. A great shadow fell upon the house and its surroundings.

INSIDE A CAR (1:30 P.M.)

"Looks like bad weather on the way," said Mori Shigehiko from the passenger seat. He was looking up at the sky through the windscreen.

"They did say a typhoon was coming," replied Mitamura Noriyuki, both hands on the steering wheel. "It's going to pour tonight all right."

The sky was dark and, since they were driving on a wooded road along a valley, mostly hidden from view. The grey clouds above blended with the shadows cast by the cedar trees around them.

Mitamura took one hand off the steering wheel and yawned loudly. Mori offered to take over.

"Should I drive? You hardly slept last night, because of that emergency patient, right?"

"Oh, no, I'm fine," said Mitamura calmly. "We're almost there. I think we'll arrive around two o'clock."

Mitamura ran a surgical hospital in Kōbe City. They had left his house at eight that morning. Mori taught art history at M— University in Nagoya, and like previous years, he'd arrived in Kōbe a day early and stayed the night at Mitamura's.

Some Western music that Mori had never heard before was playing on the car radio. Mitamura said it was German progressive rock from the seventies. Mori didn't particularly care for the genre, and it had been a long ride, so the music was starting to get on his nerves. But he couldn't tell Mitamura that. He knew the surgeon would make fun of him if he said he didn't get this kind of music.

Mori was forty-six years old. Ten years had passed since he'd been promoted from Associate Professor to Professor. One could say that already reaching the level of professor in your mid-thirties was impressive, but his promotion was only partly due to his expertise and accomplishments. His father, the late professor emeritus Mori Fumio, who'd passed away seven years ago, had been hugely influential.

"I hope we'll be able to see *the* painting this year," Mori said, taking off his black-framed spectacles. "You've never seen it, right?"

"Sadly enough, not even once."

In truth, Mori did not really like the surgeon. Mitamura was tall and handsome, and women liked his charming personality. He was a talented surgeon and a smooth talker.

Mori on the other hand was short and stooped. He hadn't been particularly handsome to begin with, and then two years ago he'd started having hearing problems which meant he had to wear a hearing aid in his right ear. It was a small sound amplifier attached to the arm of his spectacles. He'd dedicated his life to his studies, so playing the occasional chess match was the closest thing he had to a hobby. Comparing himself to Mitamura, who was ten years younger, always made him feel inferior. But this was strengthened by animosity. How could someone that young truly comprehend the paintings of Fujinuma Issei?

"By *the* painting, I assume you mean Issei's elusive last work, *The Phantom Cluster*," mumbled Mitamura, stroking his chin. "I heard your late father actually saw the painting himself?"

51

"Yes, he saw it in Issei's atelier just after it had been finished. It was autumn 1970, the year before Issei passed away. It's a large painting, apparently slightly different in tone compared to his other works, and quite curious. But that's all I've heard," the professor explained.

"And the public never got to see it," sighed Mitamura. "Issei fell ill soon after finishing it, and it stayed somewhere in his house in Kōbe after his death. It's what he wanted, apparently. And then Kiichi took it with him to that house…"

"Well, it's the painting we all want to see. I hope he gives us permission."

Mitamura frowned.

"I wouldn't get your hopes up. You know as well as I do that Kiichi can be pretty hard-headed. If we pressure him, he might even decide to cancel the annual exhibition altogether."

"He's not an easy-going person, that's true."

"I don't like to speak ill of the man behind his back, but if I'm being totally honest, I'd say he seems rather pathetic. I think he's self-conscious and has an inferiority complex. But I guess you can't really blame him."

Miserable, self-conscious, an inferiority complex? Mori didn't quite know what to say to Mitamura's harsh words, so he just nodded. Maybe that was the best way to describe Fujinuma Kiichi.

Mori and Mitamura both knew about the accident of that winter twelve years ago. So did the other two people on their way to the house: Ōishi Genzō and Furukawa Tsunehito. It had happened on Christmas Eve in 1973, after a party given at the Fujinuma residence in Kōbe. Fujinuma Kiichi was driving two friends back home when he lost control of the car on the frozen road, causing a major accident: a frontal collision with a lorry

52

coming the opposite way. The car went up in flames. One of the two friends died and Kiichi himself suffered severe injuries to his whole body.

It had been an awful sight, Mitamura had told Mori. The gravely injured Kiichi was brought to the hospital run by Mitamura's father at the time. Mitamura had only recently got his degree, so he'd been there during the operation as an observer.

They hadn't even known where to start. The bones in Kiichi's legs had been crushed. His hands were hideously burnt, and his face was so covered by burns and lacerations it was practically unrecognizable. It was clear that even state-of-the-art plastic surgery wouldn't get rid of all the scars. Eventually, Kiichi's legs healed enough that he could manage to walk with crutches, but the injuries to his face and hands would leave cruel mementos forever. Kiichi suffered, lamented and raged at this bitter fate.

Thus Kiichi had his mask made. A mask to hide his face and allow him to retreat from curious gazes.

That expressionless white face... Mori still couldn't suppress a shudder whenever he saw it. The thin rubber mask covered Kiichi's whole head and could be tied tightly using the string in the opening at the back. It had been specially made, using his face before the accident as a model. Kiichi owned dozens of masks.

After his discharge from the hospital, Kiichi sold off his successful business. Using part of his enormous fortune, which also included his father Issei's legacy, he had that bizarre manor built deep in the mountains in the north of Okayama Prefecture. Then he started to gradually buy back all of Issei's works across the country. Within three years, he had got his hands on almost all of them.

The art world had dubbed it the Fujinuma Collection. Every connoisseur with an interest in Issei's works drooled over it.

However, Kiichi had retreated to his hidden home to get away from the outside world. He had no intention of exhibiting his collection.

Now, the four of them—Mori, Mitamura, Ōishi and Furukawa—were the only people allowed to visit the house and view the collection, once a year on 28th September, the day Issei had died.

It was already a strange arrangement: the masked man living deep in the mountains in his strange mansion; his priceless Fujinuma collection, in which Issei's elusive last work was hidden somewhere. But what made the situation even more curious was the presence of that beautiful woman.

Mori stole a glance at Mitamura.

"What do you think of Kiichi and that Yurie?"

A shadow crossed Mitamura's face.

"To be honest, I don't like what's going on there."

"I heard they got married three years ago," the professor said.

"I think it's absolutely repulsive. He's kept her locked up in that house since she was a child. The girl probably doesn't even know what marriage really is. She was forced into being his wife."

The surgeon hesitated, and then blurted out: "You know, his spinal cord didn't emerge unscathed from that accident twelve years ago. So down there…"

"Aha." Mori nodded gravely. "I see what you mean."

"Of course, it's not our place to get involved with their private matters. For now, we should just be grateful he's willing to invite us once a year so we can look at the paintings."

Mitamura shrugged and concentrated on driving. Mori pushed his spectacles back up his nose in a nervous gesture, then settled back deep in his seat.

After a light lunch, the masked master of the Mill House and his friend, Masaki, stayed in the dining room. Yurie had barely touched her food and only had a few sips of her juice, then had gone back to the tower room.

Kiichi had a few cups of coffee before he lit his pipe. Masaki was reading a book in silence.

"Oh, sir, that pipe again!" Negishi Fumie shrieked the moment she walked into the circular room. She'd come through the eastern double doors, which connected to the Northern Gallery. "Of course it's your own body, sir, so you may think me presumptuous, but you really have to take better care of your health."

When her master didn't reply and kept on puffing away in silence, Fumie spoke even more sharply: "Did you take the medicine after your meal?"

"Yes."

"Don't forget to take it after supper too, you hear me, sir?"

Then she opened the cupboard beneath the stairs and pulled out the vacuum cleaner.

Masaki looked up and asked: "Are you going upstairs?"

"Yes, to clean. Are you having piano lessons today too?"

"No, we'll have a day off today."

"I see. The guests will be here soon, so I'll have to get a move on."

Fumie was already on her way towards the stairs when Masaki called out:

"By the way, Yurie mentioned just now that there's something wrong with the balcony door upstairs."

Just then they heard the sound of an approaching car. The doorbell rang a moment later.

"It looks like the first guest has arrived," Masaki said.

"Hm."

Kiichi laid down his pipe and placed his hands on the armrests of his wheelchair. Kuramoto, who'd been standing ready against the wall, immediately went out to welcome the guest. He moved unusually quickly for his size.

"We should go and greet them too," Kiichi said.

"I'll push," Masaki offered. He got up from his seat and went to the wheelchair. Kiichi turned to Fumie and asked her to tell Yurie to come down. Fumie nodded assent as she hauled the vacuum cleaner towards the stairs.

"And please put that pipe away," she pleaded with her master again.

With the sound of Fumie's heavy tread on the stairs fading behind them, the masked master of the house and his friend followed Kuramoto to the Western Gallery and walked down it. Fujinuma Issei's works hung on the right wall, with Kiichi's study and sitting room opposite. The entrance hall was through the large door at the end of the gallery.

Kuramoto had already opened the heavy entrance double doors, welcoming their first guest into the hall.

"Thank you," the guest said in a deep voice as he bowed to Kiichi. "I'm glad to see you in good health. I'm grateful to you for inviting me this year too."

They glimpsed a black minicab beyond the open doors, making a U-turn on the other side of the bridge.

"Am I the first one? Did I arrive too early? Oh, but it's exactly two o'clock now. And who might this gentleman be?" asked the guest, noticing Masaki.

"This is an old friend of mine," Kiichi explained.

"How do you do? I'm Masaki Shingo. I'm staying here for a while."

56

"Oh, err, nice to meet you."

The guest seemed surprised. He studied Masaki's face with evident interest.

"The name's Ōishi Genzō. I'm an art dealer based in Tōkyō and was acquainted with Fujinuma Issei for a long time. So you're a friend of Kiichi's. But I have the feeling we've met before...?"

"No, I'm sure this is the first time."

"Really?"

Ōishi was a stout middle-aged man with a ruddy face. He was wearing a white shirt with a gaudy necktie, and his clothes seemed too tight on him. He had a short neck, a potbelly and a receding hairline. The little hair left on his head was sticky with pomade.

"The other guests will be here shortly, so I'll show you your room. Your bag, please," said Kuramoto, sticking his right hand out.

"Oh, thank you."

Ōishi wiped his feet on the doormat and handed his brown travelling bag to the butler. Then he turned to Kiichi. His face was sweating, but he was smiling, ready to butter up his host.

"It would please us so much if this year, you could finally show us that painting."

"*That* painting?" Kiichi repeated.

"Oh, surely you understand, Issei's final work..."

The master of the house crossed his arms in disappointment. He glared up at the art dealer from under his white rubber mask.

"Ōishi. I am quite certain I have made myself clear on this matter on more than one occasion. I have no intention of ever letting you see that painting."

Flustered, Ōishi licked his thick lips and said: "Oh, no, well, yes, you did say that. Ah, I won't insist, of course. I just..."

At that moment, Yurie stepped timidly into the entrance hall from behind Kiichi and Masaki.

"Oh, it's the little lady—no, I mean, your wife. Hello, thank you for having me today," Ōishi said loudly as he quickly stole a glance at Kiichi. Yurie's pink lips remained closed, and she only bowed the smallest amount. Masaki Shingo looked out of the front doors with an air of interest.

"I think the next guests have arrived."

The sound of a car engine could be heard above the rumble of the mill wheels and the splashing of water. It wasn't the minicab—that just had left. Ōishi went to the doors and looked outside.

"That's Mitamura's BMW. Professor Mori will be with him, I assume."

Moments later, Mitamura Noriyuki and Mori Shigehiko made their way across the bridge over the canal. Mitamura wore a beige suit that flattered his tall figure. He quickly walked up to Kiichi and held out his hand.

"I'm glad to see you again, sir! How are you feeling? I heard you caught a cold?"

"Don't worry about my health." Kiichi didn't take the surgeon's hand. "How is your father doing?"

"He's well, thank you." Mitamura withdrew his hand, apparently unoffended. "Starting this year, he's let me run the hospital on my own, so now he's always going off to play golf. He told me to send you his regards."

Mitamura shifted his gaze to Masaki, who was standing behind Kiichi.

"That's Masaki," Kiichi explained, but Mitamura didn't seem to recognize the name.

"Masaki…?"

"I was treated at your hospital," said Masaki.

This rang a bell with Mori, who'd been hiding behind Mitamura and hadn't spoken a word until now: "Ah, you're Issei's disciple, right?"

"Oh, I remember now." Mitamura nodded. A smile appeared on his handsome face. "You were in the accident…"

Ōishi clapped his hands together and let out a cry. "I thought the name sounded familiar."

"But why are you here…?" Mitamura asked. However, at that moment a blinding flash lit up the view outside. A few seconds later the bright light was followed by a loud crash.

The thunder was so forceful that it almost broke the windows. Yurie let out a short cry and everyone in the entrance hall shuddered.

"That came out of nowhere," Ōishi gasped. "Sounds like it made landfall very close by."

Yurie had covered her ears. "It's all right, Yurie," said Masaki as he lightly patted the girl's shoulder. Kiichi saw this from the corner of his eye. Then he addressed his guests.

"Welcome, everyone. I suggest you settle in your rooms now. Then we'll have tea together in the annex hall around three o'clock, just as in previous years."

ENTRANCE HALL   (2:00 P.M.)

All three guests arrived around the appointed time. Just like last year, the first one to ring the bell was Ōishi Genzō. Soon afterwards, Mitamura Noriyuki and Mori Shigehiko arrived together again, in Mitamura's BMW.

The three hadn't changed. The portly, loud art dealer with the fake smile on his ruddy face. The handsome surgeon with the pretentious smirk who offered a handshake which I ignored. The small, stooping university professor with timid-looking eyes behind his black spectacles with their hearing aid attachment.

I was in the entrance hall to welcome them like last year, but my thoughts were much more complicated than last time. There were several reasons for this.

The matter that weighed most heavily, of course, was the incidents of exactly one year ago, incidents involving these same three men. Their presence inevitably dredged up memories of that stormy night.

In fact, the memories had made me want to cancel this year. But I knew my guests wouldn't take no for an answer.

I believed that even the nature of the house's stagnant atmosphere had changed since that night.

But these three were completely unaware of all that. They were only interested in the Fujinuma Issei paintings hanging in the galleries, and, most of all, the final painting they hadn't seen yet. The one called *The Phantom Cluster*.

The greatest cause of my anxiety was of course the man who'd disappeared from that room. Was he dead, or still alive? If he was alive, where was he hiding?

Yurie seemed to share my feelings. Even my three guests, I thought, must have had similar worries.

And then there was my unexpected guest: Shimada Kiyoshi. I reflected on my conversation with him moments before. I had ordered Kuramoto to quickly prepare a room for him to stay the night. On the surface, Shimada seemed honoured and expressed his gratitude. But then I told him which room he would be staying in.

"I hope you don't mind, but you'll be staying in the room Masaki was in," I had told him.

"Masaki… you mean Masaki Shingo, who was killed last year?"

Shimada was taken aback for a moment, but then replied that it was no problem.

"Oh, I'm not the type to be afraid of things like that. May I ask how many guest rooms you have in total?"

"Three on the ground floor, two on the first floor. Your room is on the first floor," I explained.

"And the other room on the first floor, that was the room Kōjin used last year, right? The room from which he disappeared in the night."

"Yes. I've kept that room locked ever since."

"Aha. If possible, I'd like to have a look," said Shimada, not even trying to hide his curiosity. "I don't have any intention of dredging it all up again for my own entertainment. But I imagine that you're also interested in the unsolved aspects of the case."

Interested in the unsolved aspects? I had to admit that I was. I stared at Shimada, my mouth tense.

"Naturally, I can't stop you from thinking about the case. I don't know what's got into me, but I did invite you to stay here. I can't very well change my mind now and tell you to leave. But I would ask you to at least show some restraint."

"Oh, of course, I understand you completely," Shimada said with a genial smile. "But that's quite a way to put it—saying you don't know what's got into you."

Now my three other guests were standing in front of me, all trying to read my mind underneath my mask while they spouted hollow flattery. I asked Kuramoto to show them their rooms and decided I would tell them about the uninvited Shimada Kiyoshi later.

"We'll have tea in the annex hall around three."

Moments after I'd said those words, a flash of light ran through the clouds in the dark sky, visible through the semi-circular patterned glass on the upper part of the front doors. Seconds later, there followed a deafening crash of thunder that sounded as if it would rend the mountains in two.

It was like a replay of the same day a year ago. I could feel my heart pounding in my chest at this joke of nature.

TOWER ROOM ~ NORTHERN GALLERY (2:20 P.M.)

This house—the Mill House—was conceived by the architect Nakamura Seiji, an unusual man who was considered by some a genius.

Rectangular, with high walls, the house was built deep in the mountains where no normal person would want to live. The

62

outer walls were well over five metres tall, and reminded me of the ramparts of British medieval castles.

The house within these thick walls could be roughly divided in two wings. One was in the north-western corner of the rectangle, with the tower at its centre with Yurie's tower room above. On the opposite side of the large courtyard, in the south-eastern corner, was the other wing. The two wings were connected to each other by the galleries which ran parallel to the outer walls. The north-west tower wing was known as the main wing, the other as the annex wing.

The main wing was, for the most part, where we lived. My sitting room, study, bedroom and an archive containing even more paintings were located in the Western Gallery, while the kitchen and the servants' quarters were linked to the Northern Gallery. The turbine room for the mill wheels was outside the Western Gallery, built against the western wall of the house. The turbine room was a semi-basement, because it had to be level with the axles of the mill wheels. It housed the hydroelectric generator that powered the whole house. I have no mechanical knowhow whatsoever, so I left maintenance completely to Kuramoto.

The annex was a two-storey wing, currently only used by guests. In the south-east corner of the building was a circular hall with a high ceiling. On the ground floor were three guest rooms, and on the first floor two. Originally, only the two rooms upstairs had been designed as guest rooms, but after the 28th September gathering became a tradition, beds were also moved into the three rooms on the ground floor.

Galleries extended in both directions from the main wing and the annex and joined up in the south-western and north-eastern corners of the house. The south-western corner served as the entrance hall, but there was also a small circular hall in the north-eastern corner (see Diagram 1 and 2).

I watched my three guests as they went through the door to the Southern Gallery, heading towards the annex. Yurie and I returned to the dining hall in the main wing.

"Shall we go upstairs?" I proposed, and Yurie nodded with a smile. I entered the lift in my wheelchair. The lift could only take one person at a time, so Yurie went up the stairs to the tower room.

The view out the tower room windows was dark and sinister, as if the world outside was terrified of the coming storm. The sky, clouds, mountains, the river… everything was a dismal grey as far as the eye could see.

Yurie sat down at the piano. I turned to her.

"What are you going to play?"

"I don't know many pieces…" she said, laying her fingers gently on the keyboard. Clear, soft tones floated up, a register similar to her own voice. Debussy's "La fille aux cheveux de lin".

I used to like this piece. But now the beautifully free melody pained me. Last year, Yurie had spent the spring and summer of her twentieth year living entirely within the fantasy world of this piece as played by Masaki Shingo. Perhaps that period had been the happiest of her whole life.

I would never be able to play the piano for her like that. Not like Masaki Shingo had.

When Yurie had finished, she glanced over at me, as if seeking approval. I looked down at my hands.

"A wonderful performance," I said.

It was almost three o'clock, so we went down. But something happened when the lift reached the ground floor. Normally, the lift doors close automatically, but as I left the lift they stayed open. Even when I went back inside and tried the button there, nothing happened.

"Is it broken?" Yurie asked, looking puzzled.

"I think so. Kuramoto will need to look at it."

We went through the dining room to the Northern Gallery. Yurie said she needed to go to the bathroom first, so she disappeared into the lavatory next to the stairwell room.

"Sir…" came a timid voice. I turned around to see the housekeeper, Nozawa Tomoko. She'd come in from the corridor outside the dining room.

"What is it?" I replied, slowly turning my wheelchair towards her.

"Err, well…" she stammered weakly, and looked down at her hands. She was holding a piece of paper.

"You see, this…" She shuffled forward and held the paper towards me, handling it as if it were some dangerous substance. "This was lying beneath the door of your sitting room…"

It was a sheet of letter paper, folded in four. The paper was light grey lined in black. A normal kind of letter paper. I had no idea what it was. I unfolded it with white gloved hands.

Leave. Leave this house.

"What is the meaning of this?"

I could feel my face tense up below my mask. I glared at Nozawa Tomoko, who seemed shocked herself.

"When did you find this?" I demanded.

"Just now."

"When you passed by my room?"

Tomoko said yes, but then started to fidget uncomfortably.

"No, actually, I didn't find it personally…" she corrected herself.

"Eh?"

"One of the guests, Mr Shimada, found it…"

"He did?" I had inadvertently raised my voice, which made Tomoko bow deeply in fear.

"I was heading here from the annex via the entrance hall, when I saw him coming my way from the gallery. He told me he'd found this piece of paper lying beneath the door of a room—your room."

So Shimada Kiyoshi had found this note? I was convinced he would have opened and read it.

Leave. Leave this house.

The message had been written with a black ballpoint pen, with the help of a ruler, utterly disregarding the lines printed on the letter paper. A simple way to hide one's handwriting.

Was this a threat?

Leave. Was this supposed to intimidate me? Had it been written by someone currently inside the house?

I tried my best to hide my worry as I looked back up at Tomoko.

"Did you read this note?"

"No, sir, of course not, I would never…" She shook her head vehemently.

I couldn't tell whether she was lying, but at that moment Yurie returned. She looked at us, concerned.

"Is something the matter?"

"Not at all."

I folded the paper up and put it my dressing gown pocket.

Shimada and the other three guests were already in the annex hall on the ground floor, which was slightly smaller than the dining room in the main wing. The hall was a round space with a two-storey high ceiling, and the west side looking out on the courtyard had large French windows. From this side you could also access the Southern and Eastern Galleries. The main wing, entrance hall and the galleries were all classic in style and complemented the medieval-looking outer walls. The annex, however, was more modern and painted all in white.

Cosy sofas were set against the outside wall of the round hall. Beside them on the north-east, a staircase curved up and across the back wall to the first floor. It was the only way to access the upper floor of the annex.

The four men were sitting around a round table in the middle of the room. Shimada had already started chatting with them even though he hadn't met them before. Below the windows set high in the back wall stood Kuramoto, silently awaiting orders.

"Sorry to keep you waiting," I said as I moved my wheelchair to the spot left open for me, facing the courtyard. Yurie sat down beside me.

"Thank you for coming all this way to visit me again this year."

As I went through the usual pleasantries, I studied the four men one by one. Ōishi Genzō, Mori Shigehiko, Mitamura Noriyuki. Their three faces hadn't changed since last year. But the fourth man, who sat in the seat Furukawa Tsunehito had occupied last year—he was different. He had both his hands in front of him and couldn't stop fidgeting with his fingers, as if he were drawing something on the tabletop.

"Allow me to introduce our unexpected visitor."

While I gestured towards Shimada with one hand, my other hand reached for my dressing gown pocket, feeling the piece of paper inside.

"This is Mr Shimada Kiyoshi. Circumstances have led me to specially invite him for this year."

"Nice to meet you," said Shimada, bowing in greeting.

"You said you were a friend of Furukawa, right?" Ōishi Genzō said as he scratched his large round nose. "That means you're not a total stranger."

"Are you a devotee of Issei's paintings too?" Professor Mori asked Shimada.

"Oh, not really. Although I am very interested in his work, of course," he said, slightly embarrassed.

"Oh." Mori blinked in surprise behind his spectacles and glanced over at me. "But why are you here then?"

"He's interested in what happened here last year," I explained. "He doesn't believe that Furukawa Tsunehito was responsible for everything."

The other three guests murmured with consternation.

"That's a rather bold idea," said Mitamura, stroking his chin. "I assume you decided to come here and play detective? Hm. To be honest, I can't believe Kiichi actually invited you into the house."

"Oh, err, well…"

Shimada neither denied nor confirmed the surgeon's accusation and nodded ambiguously.

Kuramoto started pouring tea. An uncomfortable silence filled the room.

Ōishi Genzō, Mori Shigehiko, Mitamura Noriyuki and Shimada Kiyoshi. I took another good look at them.

Who wrote that note? That was the only thing on my mind. Which of them was it? Why did they do it? In due time, I would have to ask Shimada for a detailed account of how he came to find it. I couldn't have him snooping around the house all by himself either. I'd have to make sure he understood that.

Ōishi Genzō, Mori Shigehiko and Mitamura Noriyuki. Any one of them would have had the opportunity to make their way to the Western Gallery, unobserved by Kuramoto and Nozawa Tomoko, in order to leave the note under my sitting room door. All three of them could be hiding something. They'd all do just about anything to get their hands on a painting by Fujinuma Issei...

Of course, someone else could have left the note. It could have been written by Shimada himself—and then he simply claimed that he had found it. It could also have been Kuramoto or Nozawa Tomoko, although this seemed much less likely. Or it could have been done by someone else in this house, someone who shouldn't be here any more...

My thoughts were suddenly interrupted by a clap of thunder.

"Oh, boy," said Ōishi as he pulled out his handkerchief from his tight shirt pocket and wiped his balding forehead. "I'm no good with thunder and lightning. It's almost exactly like last year."

"Indeed. But it started raining earlier last year. It was already raining by the time we went to our rooms to settle in," said Mitamura as he looked through the French windows at the sky above the courtyard. It looked as if heavy rain could come pouring down any second now.

"You have such a good memory," Shimada said.

Mitamura smirked and fiddled with the gold ring on his left ring finger.

"That's because it happened right as the rain started coming down."

"It?" Shimada repeated.

"Yes. Surely you heard about it. Negishi Fumie, the live-in housekeeper, fell from the tower balcony..."

"Aha," exclaimed Shimada, licking his lips. "How could I forget? Yes, I remember, that was the first terrible event to happen last year."

Negishi Fumie falling from the balcony. The spattering rain, the clap of thunder, the mill wheels turning and her long, drawn-out cry: the sounds all came back to me in a vivid rush.

Exactly one year ago, on 28th September, three guests arrived around two o'clock. A little while later, the fourth guest—Furukawa Tsunehito—arrived late during a downpour. That is when it started.

ENTRANCE HALL   (2:20 P.M.)

After the three men followed Kuramoto to the Southern Gallery, Masaki Shingo turned to his friend in the wheelchair.

"Not a bunch I'd like to get friendly with. They all seem to be hiding something. Why do you want that kind of person in your house?"

"I have already told you why," the masked master replied.

They were devotees of Issei, entranced by the Fujinuma Collection Kiichi had assembled, but that was not the only reason. In one way or another, the three men were all connected to the Fujinuma family.

Ōishi Genzō was an art dealer who used to handle many of Issei's paintings. Mori Shigehiko was the son of the art historian who first recognized the artistic value of Issei's works and made him famous. Mitamura Noriyuki would inherit the hospital where Kiichi and his two friends had been treated after their accident twelve years ago.

So Kiichi could not simply ignore them when they kept contacting him regarding the collection.

"But there must be lots of other people who want to see Master Issei's paintings. Have you never considered exhibiting the paintings to anyone else?"

"Never," Kiichi answered resolutely, shaking his head. "This is simply a way for me to make amends."

"Amends? What do you mean?" Masaki asked, puzzled.

"Something to ease my conscience."

As his son, Kiichi did feel some slight guilt at keeping Issei's legacy all to himself. So he showed the paintings once a year to these four men, to ease his conscience at least a little. And that was all there was to it.

"And that Ōishi mentioned something about a particular painting. Master Issei's final masterpiece…"

"That's a completely different matter." Kiichi's voice suddenly had an edge. "Have you ever seen the painting?"

"No. It didn't seem like Master Issei liked it very much. I don't think he really wanted to show it to anyone, and then right afterwards he fell ill…"

"Ah, yes."

The masked man looked slowly across the entrance hall. Several paintings hung from the shadowy walls.

"I suspect even my father never fully realized why he painted it in the first place. He seemed really troubled, perhaps even afraid of it."

Kiichi thought Fujinuma Issei had truly been capable of fantastic visions. His art had succeeding in perfectly reproducing the images of his mind, which is what led to his worry and fear at the final picture, the scene he'd put down on canvas.

"What was he afraid of?" Masaki asked, but Kiichi shook his head.

"Maybe I'll tell you one day. Not today. But…"

"Yes?"

"I'm just as afraid of that painting as my father was. You could even say I detest it. That's why I've kept it hidden. I don't want to show it to anyone and I don't even want to look at it."

Masaki didn't push the matter further.

72

"Your last guest to arrive is a Buddhist priest, right? A Mr Furukawa?"

"Yes. He's the deputy priest of the Fujinuma family temple. He's getting the boat over from Takamatsu today."

"The deputy priest? Is he the son of the chief priest?"

"Yes. His father was friends with my father."

"Ah, I see. How old is this man?"

"About the same age as you, I think. He's still single."

"Single, huh?" Masaki muttered as he looked at the cat's eye ring shining faintly on his left ring finger.

"Sorry, I shouldn't have said that," Kiichi added, realizing he'd touched on a sore spot.

"No, it's fine."

Kiichi looked away from Masaki and towards Yurie. She was leaning against the wall, looking silently at the floor.

"Furukawa will be here shortly, I'm sure. It's more convenient if I stay here to wait for him," said Kiichi, turning back to his friend. "What will you do?"

Masaki glanced at his wristwatch. "I'll wait in my room. Shall I join you for tea?"

"If you wish."

"All right. And Yurie?" Masaki asked.

"Will you wait with me?" Kiichi asked her. She nodded gently.

"Should I ask Kuramoto or Negishi to bring you some tea here?" Masaki asked.

"No, thank you," Kiichi declined the offer.

"OK, I'll see you later then."

After Masaki had left via the Southern Gallery and gone towards the annex, Kiichi let out a hoarse sigh and moved his wheelchair to the wall.

"Yurie, you don't need to stand. Sit down."

"OK."

Yurie sat on the stool next to the front doors and looked quietly out the windows on the other side at the courtyard.

The wind was blowing hard through the bushes and making waves on the pond in the centre of the courtyard. It reminded her of a restless sea.

KITCHEN ~ DINING ROOM   (2:45 P.M.)

After showing the three guests to their rooms, Kuramoto Shōji passed through the Eastern Gallery and the small north-eastern hall, making his way back to the main wing.

He was wearing a grey three-piece suit with a navy-blue necktie. His thin hair, streaked with grey, was combed back with pomade. Occasionally he'd wear something else—a boiler suit to perform maintenance in the mill wheels' turbine room, for instance. Yet he always thought he looked his best in a three-piece suit.

Kuramoto was proud to be a butler, and felt much sympathy and compassion for his master who lived so far away from civilization. He found great satisfaction in his work, managing this large mansion for his disabled employer. Sometimes this sense of satisfaction would swell out of proportion, making Kuramoto feel like he himself was the true master of the house. All told, he was extremely pleased with the job.

However, he always kept these feelings to himself. He believed that the perfect butler should be loyal, attentive, emotionless and silent.

It was his task to ensure the house remained without the smallest imperfection or error. At the same time, he'd never make

74

unsolicited comments on his master's words or actions. A servant should always maintain a proper distance.

Kuramoto stepped into the kitchen and checked the teacups laid out in advance. The fourth guest, Furukawa Tsunehito, hadn't arrived yet. The ferry from Shikoku had probably been delayed because of the typhoon. But even if he arrived late, the three o'clock tea would probably continue as scheduled.

Kuramoto glanced inside the kettle and noticed the water wasn't boiling. And he'd told her explicitly to make sure it was ready! He clicked his tongue as the face of Negishi Fumie flashed through his mind. Was she still upstairs, cleaning Madam Yurie's bedroom?

Then he remembered that Masaki Shingo had mentioned there was something wrong with the balcony door in the tower room.

Fumie simply wasn't suited for this job, he thought. She was cheerful and kind, of course, but her constant chatter made her prone to small mistakes. He'd worked with her for a long time now and it wasn't the first or even the second time he'd had to cover for her.

It was ten to three. If he put some water on right now, he'd still be in time for the "around three o'clock" tea Kiichi had ordered for his three guests.

Kuramoto topped up the electric kettle and then quickly stepped out of the kitchen. He checked his watch, which said 2:52 p.m., and made his way to the dining room. Fumie would need to come down now or they'd be late.

Lightning lit up the sky outside, followed by a thunderous explosion seconds later. Heavy rain started to pour. The whole building was enveloped by the sound of rain, lightning and booming thunder, so for a moment Kuramoto felt as if he had been sucked into another dimension.

He made a mental note to get a towel ready for Mr Furukawa, who would be arriving in the rain. He swiftly glided across the faded scarlet carpet and entered the dining room.

He was going over to the stairs when his eyes fell on the lift with the brown steel doors. Installed in the wall next to the lift were a panel with the call button and a display showing the lift's current position. He noticed that the light indicated floor "1", showing that the lift was up in the tower room on the first floor.

"Fumie?" Kuramoto called out from the bottom of the stairs. "Fumie!"

There was no answer. Was the rain drowning out his voice?

Kuramoto took a few steps up the stairs. He was about to call out for the housekeeper again when suddenly a sharp sound cut through noise of the rain hitting the house. A shrill voice… a cry!

He instinctively glanced outside through the windows across from the stairs. Perhaps it was a coincidence, or perhaps some kind of supernatural force was at play, directing his eyes. He would have believed either explanation.

For in that instant, the lightning flashed again like a strobe light, and Kuramoto saw it. Something fell through the air on the other side of the window.

If not for the extraordinary natural lighting, Kuramoto would have only seen a blurred black object. But his eyes had captured the scene outside perfectly.

He'd seen an upside-down face. Eyes wide open. Cheeks tensed up like gills. Wet hair whipping around, and a gaping mouth…

The next moment, there was a tremendous thunderclap. And then there was nothing outside the window.

Kuramoto cried out and ran over to the window. Was that… Fumie? If she was… if it hadn't been a trick of the weather, then something horrible had happened!

He stuck his head out of the window and looked down. The two-metre wide canal ran along the western outer wall at the foot of the tower. Rain was falling into the water like a hail of arrows. It was already dark outside despite the early hour, but even so Kuramoto could see a white shape bobbing about in the flowing water.

Yes, he was sure. It was Negishi Fumie in her apron.

Was she unconscious? Or was she dead? Her body seemed completely limp, bobbing up and down in the fast-flowing current.

"Oh, no!" Kuramoto cried out with trembling voice as he flew towards the Western Gallery and the entrance hall.

"Help!"

It was the first time he had shouted that loud in a decade.

ENTRANCE HALL   (2:52 P.M.)

A blinding flash was followed by a low rumble of thunder, then all of a sudden rain started pouring from the cloudy sky.

Yurie, who was sitting on a stool next to the front door, hugged herself and shuddered. Fat raindrops were punching hole after hole in the surface of the pond in the courtyard.

The silence between the couple was broken when they heard the sound of a car outside.

"That must be him," Kiichi muttered and turned his wheelchair towards the doors. Yurie got up, went ahead of Kiichi and reached for the decorated golden door knob. When she opened the door, the sound of the rain grew much louder. Flickers of lightning periodically lit up the dark sky.

A yellow cab had stopped on the other side of the bridge over the canal. Furukawa Tsunehito's shaved head could be seen through the backseat window.

"Yurie, take him an umbrella," Kiichi ordered as he moved his wheelchair outside beneath the porch. Yurie immediately disappeared and came back with a big black umbrella.

The cab door opened. Furukawa had apparently made up his mind to run for it. Before Yurie could even open the umbrella, he came flying over to the house, clutching a coffee-coloured bag to his chest. His face hung down as he made his way through the waterfall of rain.

"What rotten luck…" Furukawa muttered to himself.

It had only taken a few seconds for him to make it across the bridge and up the slope, but he was already soaked and shuddering all over.

"Forgive my miserable entrance," he apologized, bowing deeply to his host.

"Don't give it a thought. I'll have a towel brought immediately," said Kiichi. But then it happened.

The rain, the wind, the water flowing under the bridge, the three mill wheels turning powerfully as they churned the water, the cab driving off… distinct from all of these, they heard a long, shrill scream. At the same moment, lightning cut through the sky, followed by a clap of thunder.

"Did you hear something?" asked Furukawa Tsunehito.

"Indeed," replied Kiichi, looking around him. "Yurie, did you hear something?"

Yurie nodded slowly, looking pale.

"I think it was a scream…" said Furukawa, a tense expression on his face.

Suddenly a loud voice called from inside the house.

"Oh, no!"

"Who is that?" Kiichi turned around in surprise.

"Help!" came a second cry. It sounded like Kuramoto. Kiichi

78

knew right away there was something terribly wrong. But what could have happened? A few seconds later, Kuramoto came stumbling into the entrance hall.

"Sir, we have to help her." The usually imperturbable butler was visibly distraught. "It's Fumie, she's…"

"What happened to her?" Kiichi asked.

"From the tower… she…"

"What is it!"

"She fell in the canal and is being swept away!" cried Kuramoto, leaping outside into the rain and heading towards the turbine room against the western wall of the house.

The turbine room was a rectangular box, sunk halfway into the ground. Next to the steel doors on the south side, there was a ladder leading to the flat roof. Kuramoto flew up the ladder despite the heavy rain.

"Be careful!" Furukawa cried out to the butler as he ran after him. Then he went to the bridge and leaned against the railing, looking over at the ceaselessly revolving mill wheels.

"Oh… Aaaaah!" Furukawa exclaimed. He had seen something white caught in the huge, crashing black wheels.

The mill wheels kept on turning, and this time they scooped up not only water but the white object too. For a second, the housekeeper's powerless body was thrown into the air, before it fell back down once more.

"No!…" Yurie cried weakly from Kiichi's side.

"Negishi!" Furukawa wailed from the bridge.

Kuramoto called her from the roof of the turbine room too, but all their voices were lost in the relentless rain.

Negishi Fumie's body was caught once again in the merciless revolution of the mill wheels and devoured by the water. Moments later a white apron was spewed out and sent bobbing along in the swift current, speeding beneath the bridge where Furukawa was standing before disappearing into the darkness.

ENTRANCE HALL ~ TOWER ROOM   (3:20 P.M.)

Drawn by the commotion, Mitamura, Mori, Ōishi and Masaki came running into the entrance hall one after another. The rain was getting even heavier, and the wind was blowing it beneath the porch, so that Kiichi and Yurie were as drenched as the two men who'd run outside.

No one even tried to go after Negishi Fumie. She was beyond saving and everyone had realized it. The rain was just too heavy, and the water in the canal flowing too fast.

Kiichi grunted and urged everyone to go back inside. When the front doors closed, the cacophony of noise outside finally stopped.

"Kuramoto, call the police," Kiichi ordered the dripping wet butler.

Looking for Fumie in this storm would be almost impossible. Even if they did find her, it was far too late to save her now. The butler ran to the dining room for the telephone.

"What happened?" Masaki Shingo asked, panting after his run.

"Kuramoto said Fumie fell from the tower balcony," Kiichi muttered in explanation. "An unfortunate accident."

They didn't know what had happened yet, but Fumie had gone upstairs to clean the tower room, and somehow—perhaps scared by the lightning—she had fallen off the balcony. Kiichi was trying to figure out what could've happened when Furukawa Tsunehito addressed him.

"I'm terribly sorry. I wasn't able to do anything for her."

"Don't blame yourself."

80

He was right—Furukawa had nothing to blame himself for. There was nothing anybody could have done to save the poor housekeeper.

Kiichi then spoke to everyone in the room: "We shouldn't stay here. Go back to your rooms. The police will know what to do next."

His blank mask made Kiichi look calm, but his trembling voice betrayed him.

"Yurie, you're soaking wet too. You'd better change—" Kiichi started, but when he turned around to his young wife, he realized she'd have to go up to the tower room to get changed.

He turned to Masaki: "Can you accompany us? We'd better have a look at the balcony ourselves."

"Sure."

The other four guests slowly retreated to the annex. Kiichi, Masaki and Yurie returned through the Western Gallery to the dining room.

There they found Kuramoto, who had just hung up the phone and addressed his master in his usual, composed manner.

"Sir, the police are on their way. They'll also start searching the river downstream."

"Thank you."

"However..." the butler began.

"Yes?"

"There's only a small regional police station in A—, and it will take longer for the main investigation team to arrive from the nearest city. And of course it takes about an hour to get here from A— and longer as the roads are bad because of the storm."

Kiichi grunted as he moved his wheelchair into the lift.

"Anyway, you change out of those wet clothes and then get our guests something warm to drink."

"Understood."

When the lift arrived in the tower room, the first thing Kiichi did was to take a look at the balcony. Then he turned to Masaki and Yurie, who'd come up the stairs.

"You said there was something wrong with the balcony, didn't you?" Kiichi asked Masaki.

"Yes, Yurie told me so."

"You did?"

Kiichi turned to his wife. Yurie stood motionless, unconsciously stroking her wet hair.

"…Yes. The door. It creaks really loudly."

The door in question had been left open, and the howling of the wind filled the room. Masaki quickly stepped over to it and moved it back and forth. It made a nasty creaking noise.

Yurie disappeared into the bathroom to change her clothes. Kiichi went over to Masaki.

"What does it look like outside?"

"I'll have a look," said Masaki and stepped out into the heavy rain. Careful not to lose his balance in the strong wind, he slowly checked the balcony. Then he tested the steel railing.

"But this is…" he exclaimed.

"Is there something wrong?"

"Yes. This railing is unsteady. The bolts keeping it fixed in place are all loose."

A flash of lightning turned the dark valley bright as day for a moment.

The masked man closed his eyes and gasped. He cursed the storm that had upset his peaceful life. Deep within his restless mind, he mourned the death of the talkative housekeeper who'd been at his side for the last decade.

ANNEX HALL   (3:45 P.M.)

"But the police didn't manage to get there that same day, right?" Shimada asked.

"No, they didn't. They called the house back about an hour later, I think," Mitamura said in his smooth voice.

He shot me a questioning glance. I nodded back with my shiny brown pipe in my mouth and signalled to Kuramoto with my eyes, telling the butler to explain for us.

"Part of the road had collapsed in the rain. The storm was only getting worse, so there was nothing they could do until the weather improved."

"So the cab that drove Kōjin here must've made it back just in time," Shimada mumbled to himself, turning back to Kuramoto again. "And I believe they found Negishi's remains three days later?"

"Yes."

Shimada had not intentionally directed the conversation down this path, but one way or another, they'd started to go over the events surrounding Negishi Fumie's death again. This seemingly aloof man had somehow taken every person there with him in following his interest.

"We were told she'd been caught in a fallen tree downstream…" explained Kuramoto, but Shimada immediately fired another question at him.

"Did you confirm the identity of the body?" His fingers were still moving around on the table.

"I went in the master's place," the butler replied.

"If you don't mind, could you tell me the state of her remains?"

"I…" Kuramoto fell still and looked at me.

"Answer the question," I said and Kuramoto turned back to our uninvited guest who'd now taken on the role of detective.

"She looked absolutely awful."

"In what way?" Shimada pushed.

"You see, she'd been in the water for a long time by that point, and the fish in the river, they had fed on her…"

"Aah, I understand," Shimada cut Kuramoto off with a light wave of his hand. Perhaps he was thinking of Yurie. She was sitting next to me, looking down at the table.

"And the clothes she was wearing were hers?" Shimada changed his question.

"Yes. The fabric been torn here and there, but I was sure those were her clothes."

"What was the cause of death?"

"She drowned, they said."

"That means she was still alive when she fell from the balcony and into the canal. Hmm…" Shimada took a chocolate from the plate and tossed it into his mouth. He flattened the silver wrapper and started folding it. I realized he was doing origami.

"What is it you're angling for?" Ōishi Genzō asked as he watched Shimada's hands. "The housekeeper, Fumie, she died in a tragic accident."

"An accident, eh?" Shimada muttered softly to himself. "A balcony railing with loose bolts. Rain, lightning and strong wind. Yes, I suppose the circumstances do indicate an accident. Yet that's what bothers me. The circumstances seem suspicious."

"Suspicious?" Ōishi exclaimed, his eyes wide. "Are you suggesting it wasn't an accident?"

"I think that there's a significant possibility that is indeed the case."

"But that would mean it was a suicide… or murder?"

"A suicide seems very unlikely. Why would she commit suicide on that specific day? I was of course thinking of murder."

"But…" Ōishi protested.

"Well, if you'd be kind enough to just listen…" said Shimada, looking round at all of us.

He threw the chocolate wrapper on the table. It was now a silver crane.

"If, and I only say *if*, Negishi Fumie's fall was orchestrated by somebody, then it's very likely that they were also responsible for the murder of Masaki Shingo later that night. It seems impossible that two separate people just happened to commit two independent murders on the same day in the same place. That's a coincidence I cannot believe in.

"But what does it mean? It means that the person thought to be the main suspect in the incidents later that night, Kōjin—or Furukawa Tsunehito—has an alibi. He simply could not have murdered Negishi Fumie. And therefore, it is very unlikely that he murdered Masaki Shingo either. You see what I mean?"

"But why did he disappear from the face of the earth afterwards?" Ōishi asked.

Shimada was silent for a moment. "That is a good question. What if there was a different compelling reason, unrelated to the murder, that forced him to disappear?"

Ōishi snorted as he scratched his large, round, sweaty nose.

"Now you're just making up fantasies from whole cloth!"

"It's too early to tell if my idea has any basis in reality. But there's nothing wrong with considering the matter a bit longer before we settle on a conclusion. Isn't that so?"

"But…" Ōishi protested weakly.

"There's one thing I can't stop thinking about," Shimada muttered, looking over at me. I hadn't said a word. "I think I'm right in saying that Negishi Fumie lived and worked here for ten years, up until the 28th of September last year. That means she was the one to clean the tower room for all those years. And that must have included the balcony."

I nodded at Shimada.

"It seems highly unlikely that whatever the circumstances, she of all people, who knew that balcony like the back of her hand, would somehow slip and fall. And then the second curious death, a murder, occurs only a few hours after hers? Again, that seems too much of a coincidence."

"Misfortune never comes alone. Sometimes, coincidence creates the impossible," I said slowly. I truly believed it.

"Of course, that's very true," Shimada replied, though I had heard him softly tut with dissatisfaction. "But there is at least one matter that's still been bothering me, now that I've heard your recollections."

"Oh?"

"Could I ask you one more thing first? It's about the lift in the main wing, the one that goes up to the tower room."

What was Shimada getting at? I shifted the pipe between my lips as I asked him what he wanted to know.

"Does anyone besides you normally use that lift?"

"It was installed for my personal use. Of course, it's also used when something heavy needs to be moved."

Shimada nodded and tapped his angular chin a few times.

"That leaves me no choice but to point out that something very odd happened last year."

I was speechless. I had no idea what he was about to say.

"Didn't any of you realize it just now?" he went on. "It was only a minor detail perhaps, but Kuramoto revealed a significant fact earlier."

"He did?" I asked.

Everyone's eyes flew towards the middle-aged butler, who was still standing straight as an arrow, awaiting the next orders.

"Yes, he mentioned it before when he was explaining how he called out to Negishi from the base of the stairs."

He turned to Kuramoto.

"If I remember correctly, you said you glanced at the lift panel."

Kuramoto gave a stony-faced nod.

"And I believe you said you thought the display indicated Floor '1' when you looked at it?"

"Indeed, I did."

"Did you all hear what he just said?" Shimada asked, looking around the room. His fingers had started playing around on the table once again. "So that means the lift was on the first floor at that moment. But at that time, the only person who uses the lift—Mr Fujinuma—was in the entrance hall with his wife.

"You see why I think that's odd? Mr Fujinuma, you are the only person to normally use that lift, so whenever you are not in the tower room, the lift panel should indicate the ground floor. And yet at the time of Negishi's fall, it was stopped on the first floor. And that means…"

"… Someone besides Mr Fujinuma had used the lift to go up to the tower room, right?" Mitamura finished Shimada's sentence.

"Exactly. That is the simplest answer to this mystery," said Shimada, narrowing his eyes. "Mr Fujinuma, after Negishi had been carried away by the water, Masaki, Yurie and you went up the tower. Do you remember where the lift was stopped when you pressed the panel button?"

I cocked my head thoughtfully.

"I can't say for sure. My mind was elsewhere, you understand."

"Of course. Allow me another question then. When had you last used the lift before you went up to the tower?"

"… It would have been before lunch that same day. Masaki and I went up together and he played the piano for us."

"Before lunch? Then let me ask everyone else: did any of you use the lift after that?"

Nobody answered. Shimada looked satisfied.

"Well, that clears things up a bit. Nobody here admits to having used the lift. That leads to the conclusion that whoever it was must have used the lift for a specific reason, and they don't want other people to know they were in the lift and why.

"So when would someone have had the opportunity to use the lift without being seen? There was more than one person in the dining room after lunch for the whole time until the guests started to arrive. That means someone could only have used the lift unseen after the first guests arrived, when Mr Fujinuma and Yurie were in the entrance hall. We can narrow the time down even further. After showing the guests to their rooms, Kuramoto went to the kitchen. Someone must have taken advantage of that to sneak into the dining room and take the lift up to the tower room. And thus we can conclude that at the exact time Kuramoto glanced at the lift panel—mere moments before Negishi Fumie fell from the balcony—that person was still present in the tower room."

"So you're suggesting that someone pushed Fumie from the balcony?" Mitamura asked, a faint smile on his face.

"That's impossible!" Ōishi cried out.

"Why?" Shimada asked, unfazed.

"But you're saying… You're suggesting the person who pushed her is one of us three…"

"Yes, I suppose I am."

"But none of us could have known that Fumie would be in the tower room at that time," Ōishi protested.

"Hang on, that's not true," the handsome surgeon said coolly.

"Huh? How so?" The art dealer looked puzzled.

"Have you forgotten? You started chatting with Kuramoto while he was leading us to our rooms."

"Ah…"

"You asked him whether Fumie was going crazy in the kitchen now preparing for dinner. And he answered that she was still cleaning Yurie's room."

"Ah, now I do remember," Ōishi reluctantly admitted.

"Professor, do you remember?" Mitamura asked, glancing towards Mori. The professor with his black spectacles hadn't said a word until now and was reaching out with a trembling hand for his cold tea.

"I remember, yes, of course I remember," he muttered. Shimada had been watching the professor closely, but now he looked around the room again and continued his speech.

"So now you understand what I think, and—"

But Mitamura interrupted him.

"Shimada, one more thing first. I can't help but notice a few holes in the argument you've just presented to us."

"Holes?"

"You're ignoring several possible explanations. For example, someone who isn't here now could have been the one to use the lift a year ago. You should consider the possibility that it could

89

have been Fumie herself, or the murdered Masaki, who could have used the lift after lunch without telling Mr Fujinuma. Or there's also the possibility that someone in the tower room could have inadvertently pushed the call button for the lift."

Shimada ran his hands through his hair as he frowned.

"Hmm. Of course, those are possibilities. But even so, it makes more sense to think of the fall as a murder. Much more sense."

"You are a rather stubborn person, aren't you?" said Mitamura, raising his eyebrows.

Shimada smiled at him and shifted in his seat. He looked at everyone seated around the table.

"I wouldn't want you to get the wrong idea, so allow me to make myself clear now. I am not some pawn sent by the police. And I am certainly not hoping to make a name for myself by digging up a case the police have deemed an accident. But the truth is, I don't believe that Kōjin is responsible for the murder that occurred later that night. I know it's unorthodox, but that's the reason I came here today: to find out what happened for myself, with my own eyes and ears."

"I'm not going to tell you how to conduct yourself. But that doesn't mean you can come and treat us like we're murderers," Ōishi grunted angrily.

"I understand that I offended you," Shimada replied.

"And you sit there telling us all that looooong story," the art dealer went on, "but it just sounds like a theory to me. No, not even that. A fantasy! You won't catch any murderers like that."

"I already told you I have no intention of catching the killer. All I want to do is find out what happened." Shimada paused for a second, and then said clearly, "I want to know the truth."

Ōishi turned away with a grimace. The smile on Mitamura's face became a sneer. Professor Mori was hunching over the table, his fingers clasped around his empty cup and his legs shaking.

I looked at Yurie beside me. She'd averted her eyes from the table. I refilled my pipe and lit it with a match.

I called Kuramoto. The emotionless butler had been standing near the wall.

"Could you pour me some tea? And ask our guests if they'd like any."

"Yes, sir." He bowed and turned to the others.

Suddenly, we heard a light pattering of raindrops. Within moments it became a continuous heavy drumming. The whole house was wrapped in a curtain of rain. We all gazed up at the high ceiling of the hall or through the French windows into the courtyard.

Feeling my mind waver again, I mumbled, "So it has started. There will be a storm tonight, too."

ROOM 4 – MASAKI SHINGO'S ROOM (5:30 P.M.)

The three o'clock tea party was cancelled because of what happened to Negishi Fumie. The masked host informed his guests and told them they were free until dinner. Then he returned to his own quarters.

Yurie could not stay alone in the tower room, but didn't want to go to her husband's quarters either, so she spent her time sitting silently on a sofa in the dining room.

The sudden misfortune meant that Kuramoto Shōji now had to prepare dinner in Fumie's place. After seeing that the guests were comfortable, he retreated to the kitchen and began looking through the cookbooks he had hurriedly taken from Fumie's room.

The early evening wore on, and the wind and rain continued to howl down the valley outside. After a while, the police called to say that they'd had to turn back. Apparently the house was inaccessible due to a collapsed road. So now they were all imprisoned there together.

Masaki Shingo, Fujinuma Kiichi's old friend, had been living in a room in the annex in the south-eastern corner of the house for six months. His room was on the first floor, closest to the stairs.

The guest rooms in the annex were numbered from 1 to 5. The three rooms on the ground floor were 1 to 3, starting from the southernmost room. Those on the first floor were numbers 4 and 5.

The four annual guests were usually assigned to the same rooms, with Ōishi in 1, Mitamura taking 2 and Mori 3. Normally, Furukawa would have room 4 on the first floor, but this year Masaki was using this room, so Furukawa was assigned to room 5 further down the hall.

The guest rooms were about 15 square metres and built in the Western style. A thick moss-green carpet covered the floors. The ceilings were bare wood planks and the walls were upholstered in ivory white. Two pivot windows were set in the outside wall of each first-floor room, evenly spaced. They were rather small considering the size of the room, but each also had a spacious full bathroom.

Masaki heard a gentle knocking at the door. At first he thought it was just the wind rattling the door in its frame, but a few seconds later, the knock came again.

He had been enjoying a cigarette, sitting at the desk at the back of his room. He turned his chair around and called out:

"Who is it?"

"It's Furukawa."

Masaki could barely make out the answer, but got up and opened the door anyway.

Furukawa Tsunehito was a mild-mannered person, thin and short. He had a shaved head, as one would expect of a Buddhist priest, and the absence of hair emphasized his angular features. He was actually quite handsome if you ignored his pallid complexion.

"I hope this isn't an inconvenient moment?" Furukawa asked from outside the room. Masaki smiled and invited him in.

"Please take a seat."

"Thank you."

93

The humble Furukawa sat down in an armchair next to a small table. He was wearing a long-sleeved shirt woven from hemp and a pair of creased black trousers. A faint unfamiliar smell hung in the air around him. Perhaps it was the scent of incense.

"There's no particular reason for my visit. But with the storm and err, the accident, I didn't really like being alone…"

"That's all right, I was thinking about looking for someone to talk to myself," said Masaki as he turned his chair towards Furukawa. "Were you burning incense in your room?"

Furukawa nodded in response to Masaki's question.

"Does the smell bother you?" he asked.

"Oh, no, don't worry. You're a priest at a temple in Takamatsu, right?"

A self-effacing smile appeared on Furukawa's lean face.

"It's just a small, poor temple out in the country. But we also happen to tend to the graves of the Fujinuma family… That's the only reason why someone like me gets invited here."

"I was told your father was friends with Master Issei."

"Yes, that's true. That's how I became captivated by Issei's paintings. I've loved art since I was young and always dreamed of finding a job in that world, but of course I'm bound to being a priest, since I have to take over the temple."

"Aha," Masaki sighed understandingly.

Furukawa hunched over in his seat. He looked up at Masaki and asked: "I believe you used to be Issei's disciple…?"

"Did someone tell you about me?"

"No, I remembered your name. I'm sure I've seen some of your work before, too."

"Thank you."

"Ah, I recall now. Didn't you have a solo exhibition at a gallery in Ōsaka once? I think it was then that I…"

94

"That's a long time ago."

"But I still remember your work. Fujinuma Issei was impeccable in terms of using neutral colours to create the most remarkable fantastical landscapes, while you—how should I put it—used strong primary colours in unexpected combinations to…"

"That's all in the past now," Masaki quickly interrupted him. "It was more than a decade ago."

"Oh." Furukawa finally realized that he'd touched on a sore spot. He shuffled uncomfortably in his seat and tugged at his collar. "I'm sorry, I shouldn't have brought it up…"

"It's OK." Masaki stood up, went over to the desk where he'd been sitting earlier and picked up the pack of Hi-Lite cigarettes he'd tossed onto it.

"I assume you know I put down my paintbrush twelve years ago. I haven't worked on a single painting since."

"Was it because of the accident?"

"Yes. Mr Fujinuma was driving, but I was in that car… and my girlfriend too."

Masaki put a cigarette between his lips and sighed softly. The face of his girlfriend, Hotta Keiko, appeared before him.

"She died in the accident. Mr Fujinuma suffered injuries to his face, limbs and spine, and now he lives his life hidden in this house. And me? Miraculously I didn't have any major injuries, but I was damaged too. Badly enough that I couldn't paint any more."

"But you look…" Furukawa started to say, but Masaki cut him off immediately.

"Oh, I look fine, do I?" With the unlit cigarette in his mouth, Masaki spread his arms wide, as if to mock himself. "Well, you couldn't be more wrong. I was torn to pieces in that accident. There's no meaning to my life any more. I'm just a broken toy."

"But…"

"I apologize. I didn't mean to take it out on you. It happened twelve years ago now, and I have learnt to accept it."

Despite his words, Masaki bit his lip. He then noticed that Furukawa's eyes were fixed on his left hand.

"Does my ring interest you?"

"Huh? Oh, no." Furukawa looked away from the hand, but Masaki only smiled at him.

"These twelve years I have drifted around without a purpose. I did the complete opposite of what Mr Fujinuma has done, creating his own closed world and hiding himself away within it. A lot has happened in those twelve years… I used up every bit of the compensation money Mr Fujinuma gave me, and had nowhere to go any more. And that's why this spring, I appeared here out of the blue, pleading for help. He owes me the world. And while I don't know how he truly feels about me, on the surface he's been very generous—he invited me to stay in the house."

"Aha."

"Still, I don't have a penny left to call my own. All I have is this ring."

Masaki lifted his left hand up to eye level and stared at the large cat's eye on his ring finger.

"It's absolutely stuck on my finger. I can't get it off any more. It's been there for every single one of these twelve years. Even though I considered selling it more than once as a last resort."

"Is that an engagement ring, perhaps? And your girlfriend who passed away in the accident…" Furukawa asked.

"Yes. We were engaged to be married."

Furukawa looked away awkwardly.

Masaki lit his cigarette and sat down again.

"Let's talk about something else. Please tell me about yourself, and about your temple."

"Absolutely wonderful. Even after all this time, that's still the only way to describe these masterpieces," Ōishi Genzō said loudly.

His voice echoed hollowly throughout the cold room, off the stone walls and the high ceiling.

"It's a crime really, to have all these splendid works of art hidden away in a place like this. What do you think, Professor, and you, Mitamura?"

The three of them were in the small hall in the north-eastern corner of the house. After changing their drenched clothes and resting for a while in the annex, they had decided to have a look at the Fujinuma Issei paintings hanging in the galleries. They had started their tour in the entrance hall and proceeded clockwise. Issei's paintings were displayed in chronological order in the galleries, beginning with the oldest work at the main entrance.

Many different landscapes of varying size hung on the walls. Almost every painting Issei had ever created could be found in this collection, including his earliest sketches and rough drafts. Whatever wouldn't fit on the walls had been stored in the archive in the main wing.

"I wouldn't call it a crime per se," Mitamura Noriyuki said in reply to Ōishi's comment.

He had his hands on his hips as he looked at the paintings surrounding him.

"You see, I don't agree with the idea that outstanding art needs to be shown to as many people as possible."

Mitamura grinned and glanced at the stout art dealer as he continued:

"If you ask me, the idea that the works of people like Van Gogh or Picasso are our shared inheritance is utter nonsense.

This supposed consensus on artistic value is nothing more than a system designed to uphold an illusion. If you showed a hundred people a painting by Picasso, how many of them do you suppose would truly appreciate the beauty of his art?"

"Now you're just being a snob," Ōishi said.

"I know, I know, it's childish and completely senseless to argue about this. I am but a surgeon. I'm not an art critic or sociologist, so I can't explain this in technical terms, but I cannot believe there are more than a handful of people living in this world who are able to be as deeply touched by Issei's works as I am. I refuse to believe that the masses can even hope to experience what I do when I admire these paintings."

Ōishi seemed bored by the surgeon's eloquent speech.

"So you are quite content being one of the few chosen ones?"

"That's one way of putting it."

"And you wouldn't like to do something about Kiichi hoarding all these paintings?"

"Not unless it meant I could get them for myself."

"But then you'd be the one hoarding them," the dealer sighed.

"Indeed I would. But I'm sure that you and the professor feel the same as I do deep down."

"Errm, I don't think I do, you know," Mori Shigehiko said from a few steps behind them, pushing his spectacles back up his nose.

Mitamura was right though, he thought. All three of them would have liked to be in Fujinuma Kiichi's place; to be able to keep all these paintings for themselves. And Mori, too, considered himself one of the chosen. He believed he was one of the few people in the world who could truly appreciate Issei's works.

In the end, people are only able to think and feel within the limits of the "system", the specific culture of the society they belong to. Notions like artistic value and beauty are inevitably shackled by that system, and even the words we use are dictated by it.

The idea that one person alone can have the ability to truly understand a work of art might seem arrogant, or, like Mitamura said, even childish, but Mori still couldn't fight the feeling that he was different.

Take the painting he was looking at now. The large canvas was hanging in the back of the small round hall. At first it seemed a strange painting. A "river", or a thick tree trunk, flowed from the upper-right corner to the lower-left. Within the flow, oozing with light blues and greens, were three crooked "windows".

The three windows were portals into different worlds, rendered vividly by firm yet delicate brushstrokes. Unrecognizable animals lurked in the shadows. A sailing ship foundered, about to sink. Red spider lilies bloomed brilliantly…

An inexplicable feeling would capture Mori whenever he looked at the painting as a single landscape. The sensation was so overwhelming that he'd forget to employ the critical eye of an art historian.

Even after reading everything his late father, Mori Fumio, had written about Issei's work, and even though he applied everything he'd learned in his studies, Mori Shigehiko could not explain this feeling. At times he wanted to believe that these paintings defied "understanding" in the modern sense of the word. Issei's work was beyond comprehension. And the inexplicable sensation Mori felt was proof that he was one of the chosen.

"Professor, do you have any idea how we could persuade Kiichi to change his mind?" Ōishi asked, changing his target.

"Change his mind about what?" Mori replied. The art dealer grinned, showing his yellow teeth.

"You know, the one we haven't been shown yet…"

"Oh." Mori knew instantly what Ōishi was talking about.

"I tried raising the subject when I got here…" the dealer began.

"Without success?"

"Yes. He brushed me off right away. I wonder why he's so reluctant to show it to us."

"Mitamura said the same thing on our way here. We'd better not push it for now," Mori advised.

"I guess you're right."

Ōishi frowned and scratched his nose.

"Why is he so insistent on keeping it hidden from us?"

Mitamura had left the other two men behind and gone to the Eastern Gallery, towards the annex. Mori turned his back on Ōishi and concentrated on the painting in front of him.

ANNEX HALL (6:15 P.M.)

After his chat with Furukawa Tsunehito, Masaki Shingo went downstairs. Mitamura called out to him from a sofa in the annex hall. The surgeon was smiling.

"I could never have imagined I would see you here today. Where have you been these ten years?"

Masaki was fed up with the questions about his past, but he answered calmly:

"A gentleman shouldn't ask. I'll leave it up to your imagination."

"But you can't blame me for being curious. How could I not be interested after what happened? You were the promising young artist studying under Fujinuma Issei, and then…"

"You are a rather cruel man, I see."

"Don't misunderstand me—I'm not prying just out of curiosity. I realize I didn't choose my words wisely; I apologize. But I love your work from that time, and I actually own a few of your paintings. That's why…"

"That makes your question even crueller." Masaki sat down on the sofa and leaned forward, putting his fingertips together. "You of all people should know why I had to put down my paintbrush after what happened. Surely you must be able to figure out what happened afterwards, now that you've found me staying here."

Masaki glared at the man sitting opposite him. Mitamura played with the ring on his left hand.

"Where are the other two guests? Are they looking at the paintings?" Masaki asked.

"Professor Mori has gone off on another round, starting at the beginning again. Ōishi said he was tired, so he went back to his room."

Mitamura jerked his chin towards the corridor on the western side of the hall that led to Ōishi's room.

"You seem tired too," Masaki said.

"I do? We had an emergency patient last night, so I hardly slept and then we had to leave early this morning."

Mitamura's wide, narrow eyes were ringed by dark circles.

"An emergency?" Masaki asked.

"There was an accident. It was still fifty-fifty when I finished the operation, but there are other people keeping an eye on the patient now."

"A surgeon's work is never done."

Masaki had spoken seriously, not meaning to mock Mitamura, but nonetheless he hurriedly changed the topic.

"By the way, I was talking with Furukawa just now."

"Is he still upstairs?"

"Yes. I asked him if he was going to join you on your tour, but he said he wanted to go later by himself."

"Hm. He's always been like that, as if he has an inferiority complex when he's around us," Mitamura said.

"I think I understand what you mean. Just now, he seemed so self-deprecating. Talking himself down, saying he was nothing more than a priest of some unimportant country temple, that he has no talent…"

In his mind, Masaki saw the humble, spiritless look in Furukawa's eyes once again.

"… I think he also mentioned having financial problems."

Mitamura scowled and shrugged.

"A trivial thing to worry about. There are plenty of people with heaps of money who still manage to be vulgar brutes."

He seemed to be alluding to the art dealer. Masaki grinned.

"A rich vulgar brute, eh? Then I guess being a penniless one is even worse."

DINING ROOM (7:40 P.M.)

"I can't believe how terrible this storm is," said Masaki Shingo as he unwrapped a new pack of Hi-Lite cigarettes. "Will we be all right, with all this rain?"

"What do you mean?" the master of the house asked.

"I mean the house. What if there's a landslide? We're deep in the mountains and we know the road to town has already collapsed somewhere, right?"

"Aha."

Fujinuma Kiichi's reply was as expressionless as his mask. He turned to Kuramoto.

"It's Kuramoto's job to monitor these things."

"Well, Kuramoto, how do things stand?" Masaki repeated his concern.

"We've had storms like these for the last ten years," the large man stoically replied. "The house has never been damaged. You don't need to worry."

"That's a relief then," said Masaki, turning to look at the other five people seated around the table. "But it would surely be rather inconvenient for you if the storm continues, delaying the repairs to the road. I assume some of you will have to work the day after tomorrow, on Monday?"

"Things can be arranged," Ōishi said with a loud laugh. "Might as well make the best of it while we're stuck here, right? In fact, we're lucky. It means we can stay just a little bit longer to look at Issei's works."

Masaki nodded understandingly.

"Then I guess it's Mr Fujinuma who's most inconvenienced by the storm."

Everyone had gathered much later than the original plan of half past six, in the dining room in the main wing. The results of Kuramoto's arduous struggles in the kitchen had finally been served.

There wasn't much conversation during supper. Kiichi in particular was even more taciturn than usual. His silence made even the white mask seem melancholic. Ōishi Genzō's raspy voice and hollow laugh was responsible for most of the noise at the dining table. Occasionally, Masaki would respond to him, but his contributions only emphasized the lifeless mood at supper.

Nobody dared to bring up Negishi Fumie's demise that after-noon. Everyone knew that the accident was to blame for this heavy silence. Everyone, that is, except for the insensitive vulgar brute, Ōishi Genzō.

"I wonder how she could've fallen off that balcony," he blurted out at one point, before falling silent when he saw the stern look in his host's eyes.

It was completely dark outside now, and the wind was still blowing and the rain still falling. It had stopped thundering for the time being, but nightfall had only intensified the raging of the storm.

Fujinuma Kiichi picked up his brown pipe from the table, and looked silently around at everyone. His gaze made his four guests sit up straight in their seats.

"I will retire for the night now. I don't feel quite right after my cold. You can view the works in the archive tomorrow."

Kiichi put his pipe in the pocket of his dressing gown and backed his wheelchair away from the dining table, using the hand rims.

"Kuramoto, please see to our guests."

"Yes, sir," the butler replied.

Kiichi turned to his young wife, who had been sitting silently at the table with her head hanging.

"Will you be able to make your own way upstairs?"

Yurie nodded gently, her eyes still on the floor. Her long hair swayed slightly.

"If you don't feel like going upstairs, you can come to my room. All right?"

"Yes, all right."

"I bid you all a good evening then."

Masaki got up immediately, moving behind Kiichi to push his wheelchair, but the masked host lifted a gloved hand to stop him.

"Don't mind me. I can get to my room on my own."

Kuramoto opened the double doors leading to the Western Gallery. After Kiichi had disappeared into the gloomy gallery, regretful sighs could be heard around the table.

"I guess we won't get to see it tonight either," said Ōishi with a wry smile.

"It?" Masaki repeated, puzzled.

Mitamura snorted.

"He's talking about Issei's *The Phantom Cluster*. Ōishi, you really don't know when to give up, do you?"

"What fan of Issei's works *wouldn't* want to see that painting?" protested Ōishi, wrinkling his nose and glaring at the young surgeon.

He turned to Masaki.

"You were Issei's disciple, right? Don't you know what kind of painting it is?"

"Unfortunately not," Masaki bluntly replied.

"But you seem quite friendly with our host. Would he happen to have told you where he keeps it?" Ōishi tried again.

"If I said I knew where it was, would you sneak off and have a look at it in secret?" Masaki queried.

"Oh, err, no, of course not," the merchant hurried to say. Mitamura started to snigger. Masaki stroked his light stubble.

"I still have to disappoint you, I'm afraid. I don't know anything about the painting either. I'm sure *The Phantom Cluster* is hidden somewhere in this house, though."

"Aha…" The dealer puffed out his large cheeks and scratched the tip of his nose.

Then, still not ready to give up, he turned to Yurie.

"Err, so, Yurie, perhaps—" he started, but he was interrupted by Mori Shigehiko.

"Ōishi. Please drop the subject."

"The professor is right," Mitamura chimed. "It's embarrassing to listen to you going on and on like this. You're making a fool of yourself. Furukawa, what do you think?"

"Err, well…" An awkward smile appeared on Furukawa Tsunehito's lean face. "I understand the desire to view that painting, of course, but…"

"Anyway, let's not fight, OK?" Mitamura's voice suddenly took on a softer tone. He turned to Yurie, whose head had been hanging lower and lower. "Please excuse us for causing a scene."

Yurie did not react. Mitamura turned back to Masaki. "By the way, you mentioned you were teaching Yurie to play the piano. Is she any good?"

Masaki forced a smile in answer to the question. "She's rather talented."

"I hope we'll have a chance to listen to you play then," the surgeon said to Yurie. She blushed and softly shook her head. He looked at her and squinted.

"You really have grown even more beautiful in the past year. You'll be twenty soon, right? Women are often at their most beautiful at your age. I envy our host…"

FUJINUMA KIICHI'S SITTING ROOM   (4:40 P.M.)

The tea party had unexpectedly turned into an investigation into Negishi Fumie's fall of a year ago. Once the conversation had ended, I told my guests they were free to enjoy their time however they wished until dinner at half past six. Meanwhile I decided to return to my quarters.

My suite in the Western Gallery consisted of a sitting room, a study and my bedroom. The sitting room, the largest and most northerly, was directly connected to the gallery by a door. To the south of my sitting room were my study and bedroom, with the latter facing the courtyard. The sitting room provided access to the other two rooms, and there was also a connecting door between the bedroom and study. The study however did not have a door to the gallery, despite adjoining it.

I moved my wheelchair over to the sitting room windows and gazed between the beige lace curtains at the courtyard, now obscured by the veil of heavy rain. From my pocket, I pulled out the sheet of letter paper that Nozawa Tomoko had handed to me earlier.

Leave. Leave this house.

I placed my unlit pipe between my lips and carefully studied the words on the note. Who had written this, why and when?

Ōishi, Mori and Mitamura had arrived at the house after two o'clock. Yurie and I had gone through the Western Gallery on our way to the entrance hall—passing by the door of this very room—to welcome Ōishi, the first arrival. I know there was nothing under my door then.

After their arrival, the four guests were shown to their rooms, while Yurie and I again returned by the Western Gallery. I hadn't seen the note then either.

Given my low line of sight when I move about the house in my wheelchair, I knew I could trust my memory. For whether I'm being pushed by someone else or moving the wheelchair myself, my eyes are usually fixed on the floor in front of me. I would have noticed if a folded sheet of paper had been slipped under the door.

After the arrival of all four guests, Yurie and I went up to the tower room and stayed there until just before three o'clock. Then we went downstairs together, which is when Nozawa Tomoko approached me. She told me that Shimada Kiyoshi had handed her the note moments before. That would put Shimada's discovery of the note around ten to three.

Assuming Shimada did not write it himself, the note was therefore slipped under the door between twenty past two and ten to three. Any of the three guests could have done it then, unobserved by Kuramoto or Tomoko. Of course, I couldn't eliminate the possibility that it had been either Kuramoto or Tomoko herself who'd left the note.

At this point, it seemed impossible for me to narrow down the list of suspects based on the physical evidence. But one thing I knew for sure: I wasn't the "culprit". The clues available to me made everyone else a viable suspect.

I looked at the sealed study room, but quickly shook my head. What if…? No, that'd be unthinkable! Absolute nonsense.

At that moment an unpleasantly sharp knock rapped at the door.

"Who is it?" I asked.

"It's me, Shimada."

I glanced at the clock. It was five o'clock exactly. After our tea I had asked him to visit me at five. Somewhat impressed by his punctuality, I told him to enter.

"Thank you," Shimada said as he quickly stepped inside and looked around the room with wonder. "What a splendid room! Very chic."

"Please take a seat."

I gestured to the sofa and moved my wheelchair over to the table. I observed the lean man's face as he got comfortable.

"Allow me to get straight to the point," I said.

"Is it about that note?" he immediately asked.

"Indeed. I would like you to tell me how you came to find it. But first, I have to ask you…" I licked the lips of my rubber mask with the tip of my tongue. "… Did you read it?"

A shy smile appeared on Shimada's face. "I don't usually make a habit of reading other people's letters, of course. But you see, it wasn't inside an envelope, so…"

"So, you did read it."

"I won't deny it."

"You are rather crafty," I said disapprovingly, throwing the note on the table. "Please take another look. There's no point hiding it from you now."

Shimada silently picked up the note and looked at it carefully.

"It's a threatening note. Addressed to me," I said.

"But, Mr Fujinuma, why is the note telling you to leave?" Shimada asked.

It was an obvious question. I sat in silence, and he went on. "Forgive me for intruding, but do you have any idea why anyone would want to threaten you?"

"I haven't the faintest idea," I muttered, before going on in an even lower voice, "Although... What if it was written by Furukawa Tsunehito, our disappearing man?"

"By Kōjin?" Shimada looked surprised.

"You are fond of mystery stories, I believe. Well, I've decided to try thinking like they do in the novels. Suppose Furukawa, who went missing a year ago, is lurking in the house right now, planning even more horrible deeds?"

I was more talkative than usual. Shimada's thick eyebrows knitted into a sharp frown.

"Even supposing that *were* true, where could he be hiding?"

"Oh, I think there might be some place."

I paused, then decided to see what exactly Shimada really knew.

"Surely you must understand what I'm getting at. You're familiar with the man who designed this house. The architect, Nakamura Seiji."

Shimada clapped his hands together.

"Aha, so you suspect there might be some kind of gimmick that even you don't know about? A hidden room or a secret passageway or something like that?"

"I only want to point out that once you start thinking about it, that's a real possibility."

"A very interesting idea, yes, highly interesting." Shimada nodded several times. He folded the note up again and placed it back on the table.

"And you want to know about how I found this note, right?" he asked.

"Yes. I suspect this is simply a tasteless joke, with no deeper meaning behind it, but, just to be sure, I would like to hear exactly what happened," I explained.

"A joke? Are you serious?" Shimada asked.

"I'd rather believe that than think there is a person in the house planning another wicked act."

Shimada peered at my rubber mask.

"I see. There's not much to tell though, to be honest. When your three guests arrived, I was having a look at the paintings in the galleries all alone. I strolled through the Northern Gallery and made my way to the Western Gallery. It was then that I noticed something light green lying under the door of this room. It caught my eye, because it looked like some kind of stain on the red carpet."

"A stain on the carpet, eh?"

I leaned forward and picked up the sheet of paper from the table.

"Did you notice anyone else in the gallery then?"

"No, I didn't see anyone," Shimada replied.

"Hm."

"Do you mind if I ask what you think happened?"

Despite my initial hesitation, I told Shimada what I had been thinking about before his arrival in my room, and explained my reasoning about the timings.

When I had finished, Shimada said: "That narrows down the time window a lot. You say the note wasn't there when you went out to greet the three guests. I agree that we can trust your memory on this point."

"Why?"

"I noticed the note immediately, because it was sticking out quite clearly from under your door. I don't see how you could have missed it if it was there when you went by, especially given your line of sight from the wheelchair."

I nodded and grunted approvingly, despite my mixed feelings.

"I agree it seems impossible to further narrow down the list of suspects at this stage. At least, not based on the physical evidence or the time frame. But what if we consider the motive? Do you really have no idea who could've done this?"

"I already told you I don't."

"All right then, let's leave it at that," concluded Shimada with a shrug.

I felt I might have already revealed too much to this man. Perhaps he really didn't make a habit of reading other people's letters, and hadn't initially read the note either. If that was true, inviting him to my room and discussing it with him like this had been a big mistake. I didn't want anyone to disturb the peace of the house by sniffing around looking for clues.

Seemingly sensing that our conversation was over, Shimada got up from his seat.

"By the way, is your bedroom next door?"

"Indeed it is," I replied.

"But there are two doors over there," Shimada said.

"The door to the right is to my study."

"A study? Oh, that's great," Shimada exclaimed like an excited child. "I'd love to have one myself one day. My home back in Kyūshū is just an old temple, so it's impossible to have my own study there... Ha-ha, but a splendid-looking Western-style manor like this should indeed have a study... Would you mind if I took a look inside?"

"Unfortunately, the door won't open."

"It... doesn't open?" Shimada asked, surprised.

I looked away from the dark-brown door.

"I don't have the key," I explained.

"You mean, you lost it?"

"Yes."

"And you don't have a spare?" Shimada insisted.

"For some reason, all the keys to the study, including the spare, have been lost. But I haven't made a new one because I seldom used the room anyway and it's a lot of trouble to find someone to get the door opened or replaced."

Shimada chuckled as he turned his swarthy face back to the study door.

"Ha-ha, how amusing. Oh, I'm sorry, I don't mean to be rude. It's just, it seems you have your own ready-made locked room here…"

NORTHERN GALLERY (5:50 P.M.)

After Shimada had left, I went into the bathroom on the north side of my sitting room. Sitting in front of the specially lowered washbasin, I removed my rubber mask and my gloves and washed my clammy face with some cold water.

The room didn't have a mirror, so I hadn't seen my own face for a long time. But every time I washed and my fingers touched my skin, I could picture my accursed appearance. I put the mask and gloves back on once more.

Whenever I was alone in my quarters, thoughts of anxiety and worry would take hold. I had discovered that the only way to escape from this endless spiral was to leave. With time I had completely adapted to life in the wheelchair, so while I was often pushed by either Kuramoto or Yurie, I had no problem moving by myself.

The frantic storm continued to rage around the house as I moved down the gloomy gallery. The sound of the wind and rain were joined by the crashing of the mill wheels, turning monotonously yet faster than usual. It sounded like the beating heart of the house.

I headed in the direction of the tower and peeked into the dining room. Kuramoto was silently setting the table. Nozawa Tomoko was probably in the kitchen.

Kuramoto straightened up and greeted me when he saw me, but I kept going, down the hallway encircling the dining room towards the Northern Gallery. In front of me to my right was the black door of the stairwell room leading down into the basement. I remembered that Nozawa Tomoko had tried to talk to me about the basement this morning. She had mentioned something about an unusual smell now and then. I told her that it must have been her imagination, but…

Nozawa Tomoko. Could she have written the note? She had the opportunity, of course. But could that dreary, timid woman really have done something so daring? I couldn't believe it.

First of all, why would she tell me to leave the house?

How about Kuramoto then? Could he have written it?

I stopped my wheelchair and looked at the courtyard through the windows in the hallway. Outside, the garden lights glowed dim in the darkness, and drops of rain pricked the surface of the pond… I could see lights in some of the annex windows on the other side of the courtyard.

I'd put the note back in my pocket after showing it to Shimada. I closed my eyes now and pictured the sheet of light-green letter paper while I considered the possibility of Kuramoto's involvement.

He would have had the opportunity. But what about a motive?

I'd had the impression for a long time that I wasn't as important to Kuramoto Shōji as the house itself. He didn't serve Fujinuma Kiichi—he served the Mill House.

In that sense, he might have harboured some ill feelings towards me. But even so, I couldn't imagine why he would have written a note like that. If he really wanted to intimidate me, he'd choose a more subtle method.

Then I turned my thoughts to Yurie, but immediately rejected any possibility of suspicion falling on her. It was out of the question. Absolutely inconceivable.

When we went to the entrance hall to welcome our three guests, I hadn't seen anything lying under my sitting room door. Yurie had been with me all the time after that. So as long I could trust my own eyes, she never had the opportunity to put the note there. Yes, I was certain.

I moved further down the hallway in my wheelchair and started to consider other possibilities. Was the "culprit" one of the guests after all?

It would certainly make more sense. There were four guests in the house, including Shimada. This unexpected guest was a less likely candidate, so which of the remaining three was it? Ōishi Genzō, Mori Shigehiko or Mitamura Noriyuki?

All three of them had equal opportunity. I couldn't exclude any of them based on the time frame. What about motive, then?

Suppose the art dealer was the one trying to threaten me. What was he hoping to gain by it? My collection, of course. Fujinuma Issei's paintings. The same went for that surgeon, and also for the professor.

But if one of them was after Issei's paintings, why would he have told me to leave the house? Wouldn't he have chosen a clearer message?

I slowly proceeded down the Northern Gallery, stealing glances at the landscapes hanging on the wall to my left. The curtains of the windows overlooking the courtyard had already been drawn. The lights in the gallery were dim and far apart, so it seemed like a dark-grey tunnel.

I thought back to the painting that had disappeared from the wall of the Northern Gallery on that stormy night last year. It had been a small painting titled *Fountain*. The piece was centred on the mystical silhouette of a fountain on a hill, against a backdrop of what appeared to be the sky moments before daybreak. When I pictured the perfectly arced lines of the water… the billowing clouds…

But it was then that amid the drumming of the rain on the windows, I suddenly heard a man whispering.

"I hope you aren't offended if I tell you that you have grown very beautiful in this last year."

The voice was coming from the small hall in front of me. The doors were closed.

"I'm so jealous of your husband."

There was no response.

"Your husband has these fabulous paintings all to himself. And he even has a wonderful woman like you at his side…"

It was Mitamura Noriyuki, without a doubt. I did not hear Yurie give any reply, but they seemed to be alone inside the hall. Silently and carefully, I approached the door.

"Oh, yes, there was something I wanted to ask you, if it's not too much trouble," Mitamura continued.

Silence.

"I'd like to have a look at the paintings in your room in the tower. I saw them the very first time I visited the house, but I'd love to see them again…"

I couldn't hear Yurie's response.

"No, keep it a secret from your husband, please. I don't think he'd like it. I also wanted to have a chance to have a talk with you alone, just the two of us. I think you'd enjoy my company; I know I'll enjoy yours. You don't mind, do you?"

Once again, I couldn't hear her reply.

"OK, that's settled then. I'll be there… just after midnight, all right?"

Oh, Yurie! The words almost escaped my throat. I couldn't see Yurie's reactions to Mitamura's honeyed words, nor could I make out her softly spoken replies, blocked by the door between us. But I could sense that at the least she had not resisted the man's advances.

Why didn't you refuse him? Why would you listen to anything he had to say?

I tried to calm my raging mind. I even considered barging in, telling Mitamura I had overheard everything.

Was this jealousy? A feeling of self-loathing suddenly rooted me to the floor.

Mitamura was right; she'd grown so gorgeous lately. No wonder the filthy surgeon had suddenly approached Yurie now, when he'd done nothing last year. But still… Why?!

Engulfed by a wave of negative feelings, I turned my wheelchair around and returned to the gloomy gallery.

DINING ROOM (7:10 P.M.)

"When did you buy this TV?" Ōishi asked, wiping a napkin across his dirty mouth. We'd just finished our meal. "It doesn't really fit the classic feel of the rest of the room."

"I bought it last autumn, after what happened," I said, looking at the large television set against the wall. "I was beginning to feel it was too... too silent in the house. That's why I decided to buy it."

Until last year, the only televisions in the house had been in the master's sitting room and the two servants' rooms.

"Mind if I switch it on?" Ōishi asked.

"Feel free."

The merchant picked up the remote control from the table and turned it on. The valley has bad reception at the best of times, and with the storm the image on the screen was even blurrier than usual.

"They're talking about the typhoon," Ōishi said, attracting everyone's attention. The programme had just started.

Typhoon 16, which had brought terrible rain and wind to the whole Kyūshū area, was now heading east, and was predicted to move out over the Sea of Japan tomorrow morning. While the typhoon had weakened slightly, people in the Chūgoku region were advised to stay on their guard, as more heavy rain and fierce wind were still expected.

"I hope the road doesn't collapse again. As I remember, the typhoon last year followed the exact same course," Mitamura said, a brandy glass in his hand.

Ōishi laughed loudly for some reason.

"Hahaha, coincidences are funny sometimes, right? Kuramoto, a scotch and water for me. And I think your master prefers it on the rocks?"

"No, I'm fine. I don't feel like drinking now," I said and put my pipe between my lips. "But please don't mind me. Shimada, what about you?"

Shimada Kiyoshi had hardly spoken during dinner, contrary to his behaviour at the tea party in the afternoon. He appeared to be in deep thought. Just like this afternoon, the fingers of both his hands had not stopped fidgeting on the table during and after dinner. Before we knew it, he'd lined up a whole series of origami models in front of him, made out of napkins and snack wrappers. They weren't the usual cranes or ships, but much more complex works of art, the likes of which I'd never seen before.

Shimada finally looked up and stopped moving his fingers. "Oh, a drink? Yes, I think I will."

Once Shimada had been handed his whisky and water, Ōishi raised his glass, indicating that he wanted to make a toast.

"Allow me the honour. To the fabulous works of Issei."

"And to our host's health, and Yurie's beauty," Mitamura added.

I glanced over at Yurie, who smiled politely, without embarrassment, at the words Mitamura had dared to say. I felt a weight in my heart. Yurie still had not confided to me her conversation with Mitamura. I hoped I wouldn't have to bring up the topic myself.

Next, Mitamura addressed Mori Shigehiko, who was sitting at the table with hunched shoulders, his head hanging.

"Professor, what's the matter? You haven't spoken a word."

"Oh, I haven't?"

Mori tried to hide his unease by adjusting his angular black spectacles with their hearing aid attachment.

I had also noticed his curious demeanour. He'd been silent both during and after dinner. He wasn't the talkative type in general and didn't drink much, but it was obvious something was weighing on his mind. He'd seemed out of sorts during the tea party, too.

"Something on your mind?" the surgeon asked again.

"No, it's nothing." The professor shook his head vaguely, but then seemed to change his mind. "Well, you see, to be honest, I don't know whether I should mention this…"

The professor shifted his gaze to Shimada, who was sipping at his drink.

"Shimada, there's something I've been thinking about."

"Oh, yes?" Shimada's eyes opened wide and he sat bolt upright. "What would that be?"

"It's about our discussion this afternoon. Regarding Ms Negishi's accident last year."

"I see. Did you remember something else?"

The professor rested a hand on his prominent forehead.

"Well, yes. But I'm not sure it's really anything important. That's why I've been hesitating to mention it to you. You said her fall might have been a murder rather than an accident, right?"

"Yes. Of course, my reasoning regarding the lift was far from watertight, as our esteemed medical man pointed out."

"Well, I remembered something while I was listening to you this afternoon. Something very trivial that I'd never given much thought to until today."

Shimada put his glass down and licked his upper lip. "Please go on—what's on your mind?"

"It was when we heard the commotion at the front entrance, and came running," Mori explained. "We heard Kuramoto's scream all the way in the annex and realized something was going on in the entrance hall, so we hurried over there. And after Ms Negishi had been carried away by the water, we went back to the annex."

Mori kept pushing his spectacles back up his nose as he talked. He was speaking slowly, as if he was telling the story of what had happened a year ago to himself, going over every part in his memory to make sure he was getting it right.

"And on our way back, I think I noticed something in the gallery," he continued.

"What did you see?" Shimada asked.

"The carpet in the gallery was wet."

"The carpet?" Shimada repeated.

"Yes. I remember noticing that the carpet in the Southern Gallery was wet when we were on our way back to the annex."

"So? What does that tell us?" Ōishi interrupted him.

"No, Ōishi," Shimada cut in, stopping the art dealer. "It's actually very… aha, I see, very interesting…"

He pursed his lips and looked back at Mori. His fingers began to fiddle on the table in front of him again.

"Professor, please continue."

"You see what I'm trying to say?" Mori asked, finally letting go of his spectacles. "I was in shock after what had happened, of course, but I still remember that I was leading the way as the four of us—Ōishi, Mitamura, Furukawa and myself—went back to the annex via the gallery. We were all soaking wet because of the rain, so there was of course nothing odd about the carpet being wet after we walked back inside. But I remember looking at parts of the carpet in front of me that were wet already, parts we hadn't reached yet."

Mori paused here and everyone in the room went silent. Somewhere far away the rumble of thunder drowned out the noise of the relentless rain.

Ōishi looked as if he was tackling a difficult maths problem. "So, that means that someone—someone soaking wet—had gone through the Southern Gallery before the four of us returned to the annex?"

"Yes, that's what it comes down to," said Shimada. "When you all came hurrying from the annex towards the commotion in the entrance hall, one of the group was already wet, or at the very least was wearing wet shoes. By 'the group' I mean of course Mr

Fujinuma's three guests who are here today, and the late Masaki. Oh, Professor, do you mind if I take over?"

"Please do," Mori said.

He'd turned pale.

"The vital question we need to ask now is: why was that person wet? Had they just got out of the bath? No, that can't be right. Unless someone can say they had been using the bath or shower at that time?"

There was no reply.

"Let's look at the other possibilities, then. For example, do any of you admit to spilling water from a vase on the floor, or to having a problem with the tap in the lavatory, or anything like that? No? Well, if they didn't have some kind of accident inside the house, then there's only one possible reason the person could have been wet: they were wet from the rain."

Shimada looked to Mori for agreement.

"Yes, that's exactly what I thought. One of us must have got wet already from the rain," the professor said.

"Which brings us to the next question: when and where did this person get wet? Allow me to ask all of you another question. Does anyone here admit to being this person? If so, give us a proper explanation, if you please."

Shimada's question however was once again swallowed up by the silence in the large dining room. He looked oddly content at this.

"Nobody. Nobody admits to being the wet person. That leads us to one conclusion. It means that person got wet in the rain, because they had been out on the balcony in the tower room. Which in turn means that the person was implicated in the fall of Negishi Fumie, which occurred just before this. No, allow me to choose my words more definitively. That

122

wet person is the murderer who shoved Ms Negishi from the balcony."

Ōishi gasped, lost for words. Mori wiped the perspiration from his brow. Mitamura gazed down calmly at his brandy glass. Shimada observed all three of them.

"There might be some other possible explanations. But at the very least, what Professor Mori has just told us now seems to add significant weight to my theory that Ms Negishi was murdered. What do you think, Mr Fujinuma?"

"It's difficult to say," I replied bluntly. "What about you?"

I directed the question at Mitamura, who snorted lightly.

"Hm. Shimada, I have the feeling that once again you are trying to convince us that Furukawa did not kill Masaki last year, right?"

"Yes, that would be correct," Shimada replied, but then lowered his voice to a near whisper. "I can't be absolutely certain, of course. But Negishi Fumie *was* murdered. And Kōjin has an alibi for that crime, as he arrived at the house exactly as it happened. And therefore, he can't have murdered Masaki either. I admit, at the moment this is not a very convincing way to disprove the many suspicions laid upon him."

"Indeed, it's not," Mitamura said.

"I simply want to point out that considering the facts surrounding the lift we talked about earlier, and now the matter of the wet carpet, we should carefully reconsider the events that occurred last year one more time. Was it really Kōjin who was behind it all? And if not, who was the real culprit?"

Mitamura shrugged and brought his glass to his mouth.

"I have no intention of taking up all of your time, but allow me to make one suggestion," Shimada said as he looked around at everyone.

No one reacted. Kuramoto, who'd been standing directly behind Shimada, against the wall, coughed at that moment. It sounded deliberate.

"Let's put the matter of Ms Negishi aside for now. What we should look at next is of course what happened with Kōjin later that night. His flight… no, I should call it his disappearance. The disappearance of Furukawa Kōjin. I know the outline of what happened, but I suggest we examine in detail, once again, the circumstances of how he came to disappear from the first floor of the annex."

NORTHERN GALLERY   (8:15 P.M.)

After her husband had retreated to his quarters, Yurie also went back to her room in the tower. Masaki and the four other guests took it as a sign to return to the annex as well.

The five men entered the Northern Gallery and slowly strolled down the dimly lit corridor, admiring Issei's paintings, each of them thinking and feeling differently about the works.

Suddenly Masaki came to a halt and said: "Suppose Mr Fujinuma said he would agree to let go of one of these paintings…?"

His words stopped the four other guests in their tracks. They all turned to look at him.

"Did he say that!?" Ōishi cried out.

"I did say *suppose*," Masaki picked up with a wry smile. "I'm simply asking—what if he did say that? How much would you be willing to pay for one of these?"

Ōishi's eyelids fluttered and he practically began to drool. "It would depend on the work in question, naturally. But money would be no object for me."

"Aha. Let's take this painting as an example then," Masaki said, pointing at the small painting hanging in front of him.

"*Fountain*? From 1958, right?" The art dealer crossed his arms, eyes fixed on the remarkable landscape of a fountain on a hill.

"Fifteen million yen."

"I see. Quite the number," Masaki said with a grin. He looked at the other three men and repeated his query.

"What a boorish question," Mitamura said as he rubbed his chin.

"I am a childish man, I know. Well then, let's add a dose of reality to the scenario. What if I were to personally appeal very strongly to Mr Fujinuma on this matter? He might well sell then, because of his guilt over what happened twelve years ago."

Mitamura frowned. "Hmm. It's hard to put a monetary value on something like this. But if he was truly willing to sell this painting to me, I agree with Ōishi, money would be of no consequence."

"Professor?" Masaki asked next.

Mori made to speak, before seeming to change his mind. "Yes, I'd feel the same," he said at last.

"And you, Furukawa?" Masaki asked finally.

Furukawa shook his head noncommittally. Seeing the uncomfortable expression on his face, Masaki felt somewhat guilty for putting him in this position. Furukawa was biting his lip in frustration; he knew price was an issue for him.

"I'm guessing the price would be astronomical if *The Phantom Cluster* were up for sale, right?" Masaki cut in to spare the priest's embarrassment.

"I'd need to have a look at the actual painting first," Ōishi replied, to which Masaki spread his arms wide and looked around him.

"You would? I wouldn't think that the painting's true artistic value would matter at all if the opportunity arose to buy it."

"Excellent observation," Mitamura said. His sneer seemed to be aimed at everyone in the room, including himself. "You're absolutely right, Masaki. We—no, I, at least, am transported whenever I admire Issei's works. It's an experience that you can't put a price on."

"What was that all about?"

Ōishi scratched his sweaty nose as he posed the question to Mitamura, who was sitting on the sofa opposite. The surgeon had been swirling a brandy glass in his hand, but at Ōishi's words, he stopped. The alcohol had made his eyes slightly bloodshot.

"What are you talking about?" he snapped.

"You know, what Masaki told us in the gallery. About how Mr Fujinuma might be willing to sell a painting."

A scowl appeared on Mitamura's face, as if he'd expected Ōishi to say something else.

"Don't tell me you think he's serious?"

"It's not impossible."

"Perhaps, and only if Masaki did indeed act as a middleman. But he never would. I think he was just making fun of us."

"No, but if we could somehow convince him…" said Ōishi, like a true businessman. He removed the cigar from the corner of his thick-lipped mouth, placed it on the ashtray on the table and spat into a tissue.

"He's been a guest in this house for about half a year now and we still don't know why. A stay of a month or two might be normal, but six months? Don't you think that's fishy?" Ōishi asked.

"Hmm," Mitamura mumbled.

"It certainly is. It reeks like hell. He might really need money, or maybe he's in even bigger trouble… I'd never met him before today, but I could swear I've seen his face somewhere else before. A photograph, something like that."

"A photograph?" the surgeon asked with some interest.

"I don't remember exactly any more, but it could've been the newspapers or a magazine… Anyway, we could use that to our advantage."

Mitamura snorted, then narrowed his eyes and began to play with his ring.

"Hm. Do you want to strike some sort of deal with him?"

A sly smile appeared on Ōishi's face.

"You could say that, yeah. I've always thought you can divide the people in this world into roughly two groups: those who've got money, and those who haven't. And you can tell what group a person belongs to. Reading people is what doing business is all about. And it's obvious that Masaki hasn't got a penny. You must have sensed it too. He gives off the same aura as that priest."

"That reminds me," Mitamura said. "Mr Furukawa seems especially listless this year."

"You said it. He was always like that, of course, but did you catch the look on his face when we were talking about being willing to pay millions to get our hands on a painting? The more that priest longs for Issei's paintings, the more he suffers, because he knows he'll never be able to own one himself."

Ōishi suddenly fell quiet as he heard footsteps on the stairs. It was Furukawa Tsunehito, coming down from his room. When he noticed the two men sitting in the annex hall, he stopped and nervously averted his eyes.

Mitamura had to conceal a smile as Ōishi called out to Furukawa in a friendly voice, asking him to have a drink with them. But the other man declined the offer.

"Thank you, but I wanted to have another look at the paintings…"

When Furukawa's lean, drooping figure had disappeared into the Southern Gallery, Ōishi spat loudly into his tissue once again.

"That's a depressed guy if I ever saw one."

"He does seem to be brooding over something," the surgeon observed.

"I can't stand people like him, who keep everything cooped up inside," said Ōishi.

He refilled his glass.

"… But I suggest we get a hold of Masaki later and have a good talk with him."

Mitamura's more sober gaze was fixed on his interlocutor's balding pate. In his mind, he called him a vulgar swine. Even a game of chess with the professor would have been more enjoyable than talking with this grubby merchant. The same thought crossed Mitamura's mind every single year.

ANNEX HALL ~ NORTHERN GALLERY (9:50 P.M.)

After he had finished cleaning up in the dining room, Kuramoto Shōji passed through the Northern Gallery on his way to the annex. He appeared to be his usual unemotional self, but secretly he still hadn't recovered from the shock. The face he'd seen only a few hours before—the upside-down face of Negishi Fumie on the other side of the window—had been burnt into his retina.

That expression on the face of the woman he'd lived and served with for a decade. The way she looked at the very moment before her death. Even her scream, cutting through the noise of the heavy rainfall, still echoed in his ears.

He'd seen her body be thrown in the air by the mill wheels and swallowed by the raging flood: there was no chance she'd survived. When the policeman had called to say they couldn't start their search for her yet because the road had collapsed,

Kuramoto could hear in the officer's voice that he considered it a lost cause.

His old colleague suddenly snatched away.

Kuramoto didn't think of himself as a particularly cold-blooded person, but for some reason Fumie's tragic end had not made him feel straightforwardly sad.

He did feel sorry for her. But more than that it was shock, anxiety, fear and dread that whirled about inside his mind, deeply unsettling him.

It was almost a miracle he hadn't broken anything while he was preparing dinner—a task he was not at all used to—and serving the food. Whenever Fumie's face and voice crossed his mind, his hands trembled. He did all he could to keep the images at bay.

There had been an accident, and there was nothing he could do about it now. All he could do was finish his remaining tasks for the night.

Ōishi, Mori and Masaki were sitting chatting on the sofas in the annex hall. Mitamura was probably in the bathroom. Kuramoto had heard the sound of the shower running when he passed the bathroom in the northern part of the annex. Mori's hair was still wet—he'd probably taken a shower already.

"Is there anything I can assist with? Please feel free to take any drinks you wish from the sideboard. Is there enough ice?" Kuramoto asked the three guests politely.

"Yes, thank you, Kuramoto," Masaki said. "Today must have been taxing for you. I know where everything is here, so you don't have to worry about us. Please retire early yourself."

Kuramoto bowed deeply.

"I'm very grateful. If there's anything you need, don't hesitate to call me. I've been told to tell you that you're also free to view the paintings in the galleries, but I must remind you that the lights go out at midnight, so please don't be out roaming the galleries at that time."

"You've been telling us that for so many years, I know it off by heart," Ōishi said, laughing loudly at Kuramoto's annual expla- nation of the house rules. The art dealer was already quite the worse for wear.

Kuramoto took one last look around the annex hall, and then said:

"I bid you a pleasant night."

He left the hall and quickly made his way to the kitchen. He still had a lot of dishes to wash. Once he'd finished them, he had to check the mill wheel turbine room and make sure to lock up all the doors and windows… And Fumie had told the master not to forget his cold medicine. What should he do? Oh, well, it wasn't his job to care for his master's health too.

At that moment, Fumie's face as she fell from the tower flashed before his eyes again, and he heard her long, long scream…

Kuramoto shook his head to rid himself of the image. He had just left the small hall in the north-eastern corner of the house and entered the Northern Gallery.

The storm continued to rage fiercely outside, blowing rain against the windows facing the courtyard.

Just then Kuramoto noticed a shadow about halfway down the dimly lit gallery. He flinched at the unexpected sight, but upon closer inspection the bald head told him it was Furukawa Tsunehito. He really was too thin, and looked scruffily dressed in a long-sleeved white shirt and black trousers. From afar, Furukawa almost looked like some poor, tired college student working a part-time job.

He was standing with his arms folded, looking at a painting on the gallery wall. He had not noticed Kuramoto's approach.

Suddenly Furukawa stepped forward and reached out his right hand, almost touching the painting.

It was as if he were possessed. Kuramoto could not fathom what was going on in his mind, but he could not allow a guest to go around pawing at the priceless paintings in the collection. He coughed loudly to let the young man know he was not alone. Furukawa stopped and looked around. When he saw Kuramoto standing there, he quickly pulled his arm back.

Kuramoto approached Furukawa unhurriedly.

"You are free to look at the collection, but I will have to ask you to not touch the paintings."

Furukawa's eyes were darting around in a panic. He took a handkerchief out of his trouser pocket and mopped his forehead.

"Oh, err, of course I wasn't... I mean, the painting was so mesmerizing, it was instinctive..."

"I repeat, I must ask you to be careful not to touch the paintings."

"Yes, of course, I understand."

Furukawa's bony cheeks had turned red. Kuramoto knew it was from shame, not anger.

"Thank you very much," he said and walked on. He could hear a soft sigh escape from Furukawa's mouth as he passed.

When Kuramoto reached the kitchen, he turned around. Furukawa's stooped figure was still in the same spot; he hadn't moved an inch. He was staring at his feet, but Kuramoto could see him shooting occasional glances in his direction. This worried the butler, but he couldn't stay and keep an eye on the man the whole night. He nodded a silent goodbye and made a mental note to report this to his master later. He opened the door to the kitchen, where the unfamiliar task of washing dishes awaited him.

A light was swaying in the darkness. It was weak, and moving slowly, but it was definitely there, and it was definitely something man-made rather than a natural light source.

Kuramoto Shōji was about to close the curtains of his room on the edge of the main wing when he took another good look at the darkness outside, rubbing his tired eyes.

The servants' quarters consisted of two rooms to the east of the tower. A narrow corridor separated the two rooms from the kitchen. The northern room—the one closest to the gallery—had been Negishi Fumie's. Kuramoto's room was next to hers. His was a corner room, with two walls abutting the courtyard.

What was that light? he wondered.

It had been half past ten when Kuramoto had finally managed to finish up in the kitchen. He had then gone to check the turbine room like he did every night. Its door was in the northern section of the Western Gallery. There was another door to the turbine room outside, near the front doors, but it was almost never used.

The door from the Western Gallery led immediately into a small room with a low ceiling and a sunken floor. This room was part of the rectangular concrete building running along the outside of the western wall of the Mill House. Behind a door in the left wall of the small room were the stairs going down to the semi-basement of the turbine room.

Because the walls were soundproofed, the noise of the mill wheels was hardly noticeable in the main wing, even if you were in the Western Gallery, but inside the turbine room the noise was so loud that it sounded like a small factory. The gigantic mill

133

wheels rotated right on the other side of the concrete wall. The rumbling, the sound of churning water…

The atmosphere inside the room was far from that of the peaceful silence inside the house.

Three massive axles protruded from the house wall and spanned the room. The whole structure surrounding the shafts was metal, built to optimize strength, durability and energy transmission efficiency. Generators and transformers were dotted here and there among the machinery. Ten years ago, when Nakamura Seiji designed this building, he had called in an expert to create this gigantic contraption.

Kuramoto had been tasked with managing this room and its machines, but even he did not understand every detail of how it all worked. Still, he had studied the thick instruction manuals closely enough that he could deal with most problems that arose. In fact, over the last ten years, apart from the semi-annual inspection, he could boast that he'd only had to call in an expert two or three times, to fix problems with the generator.

He looked out at the canal through the window in the wall.

The water flow had slowed, but the storm was still raging outside. There were no lights in the front garden on the other side of the canal. Clouds darkened the night sky.

Kuramoto shuddered. This room always felt eerie at night. And this weather only made things worse.

He reached for the torch he kept in the turbine room and pointed it at the canal outside. The water level had risen a lot, but was nothing to worry about. If it got dangerously high, he'd need to go to the dam upstream and adjust the volume of water flowing into the canal, but he wouldn't need to deal with that any time soon. Next he had a careful look at the various meters. No abnormal values anywhere.

Once he had finished in the turbine room, Kuramoto went around the house to check that all external doors and windows were locked securely. He started in the tower section of the main wing and checked the whole house methodically, going in clockwise direction: the windows in the dining room, the back door at the western end of the Northern Gallery. There were vents high up on the gallery wall, but no windows to check there.

Kuramoto made his way through the small hall and the Eastern Gallery to the annex. Mitamura Noriyuki and Mori Shigehiko were on the sofas in the hall, playing chess. Masaki Shingo was sitting next to them watching the game. Kuramoto was told that Ōishi Genzō had retired to his room a few minutes earlier, accompanied by a glass and a bottle of brandy.

Thinking back to what had happened in the Northern Gallery, Kuramoto decided to ask about Furukawa. Apparently he'd turned in for the night even earlier, at half past ten.

As Kuramoto was about to leave the annex hall, he heard Masaki getting up from the sofa, saying he was off to bed too. Kuramoto happened to look at the clock just then. It was ten to eleven.

He then went on through the Southern Gallery to the entrance. He was used to locking up, but even so, he never enjoyed walking about the house all on his own. Especially not tonight, considering what had happened earlier. The fierce storm was still blowing outside. He flinched now and then at a far-off rumble of thunder.

Once he had finished in the Western Gallery, he returned to the dining room. There was nothing out of place anywhere. Everything had been locked up, and not one of the paintings in the galleries was hanging crooked—something his master had asked him to look out for, especially when they had guests.

While Kuramoto was at the sideboard preparing the nightcap he'd been looking forward to, his eyes wandered over to the windows, where the curtains had already been drawn. He shook his head to dispel the images that came flooding back again and prayed for the housekeeper who'd moved on to the next world.

It was half past eleven when Kuramoto was finally finished with all his tasks and went to his own room. After washing in the servants' bathroom next to the kitchen, he at last allowed himself to take off the imperturbable butler's mask he wore all day.

Sitting in the rocking chair by the window, watching television and sipping his whisky was usually a moment of blessed pleasure at the end of a hard day's work. But the accident made it rather different today.

After his second glass he rose on tipsy feet, switched off the lights in his room and was about to make his way to bed. But just as he was drawing the curtains of the south-facing windows, he noticed something outside. This time he knew he wasn't mistaken. There was a small yellow light shining in the gloomy darkness.

It was coming from the direction of the annex.

There were a few garden lights installed in the courtyard, but they were hardly visible in the heavy rain and strong wind.

Absolute darkness reigned outside. The shadows cast by the house had consumed all light save for the little coming from the annex hall on the opposite side of the courtyard. Mitamura and Mori were probably still busy with their game of chess in the annex hall. But the light Kuramoto had noticed was high up to his left, somewhere near the windows of the first-floor hallway of the annex.

What could it have been? Kuramoto wondered again. The lights in the first-floor hallway were off. So what was the source of the swaying light that had disappeared so suddenly?

Had someone lit a cigarette in the dark hallway? But what he'd seen didn't look like the flame of a match or lighter. It was much more like the light from a torch...

Raindrops streamed down the window as Kuramoto moved his face closer to the glass. He tried to peer into the darkness beyond, but he couldn't see anything. He could just about make out the windows of the hallway on the first floor, but there was no light to be seen now.

He told himself it wasn't worth thinking about. He was just on edge because of the events that afternoon. He was exhausted and his knees were aching, probably from sprinting down the gallery as fast as he could after the fall.

He silently drew the curtains in his room, went to bed and fell asleep.

FUJINUMA KIICHI'S STUDY   (1:15 A.M.)

He couldn't get to sleep.

He wasn't too hot. The room was cool enough. Yet still he was uncomfortably clammy beneath his underwear and around his neck. The air was muggy from the endless rain. And he hadn't taken a bath in two days because of his cold.

He would have liked to take a shower, but, with Negishi Fumie gone, even managing that would be difficult. He could get out of bed into his wheelchair and was able to dress on his own, but he didn't think he'd be able to wash.

There was no chance Fumie had survived. He'd need to look for someone to replace her tomorrow.

Kuramoto wouldn't be up to the task. He was an excellent butler, but his loyalty was not to his master. Kiichi knew that: Kuramoto's loyalty was to the house, to the building itself.

The butler was completely oblivious to any changes in Kiichi's mood or health for a start. Take Kiichi's cold. Two or three days before he got a fever, he'd developed a runny nose and a sore throat, but Kuramoto hadn't noticed anything amiss with his master's health until Fumie pointed it out to him.

Did he really need to find a new housekeeper?

Kiichi rested his elbows on the desk in the centre of the study and removed his white rubber mask.

The study was a spacious square room. There was a fireplace on the gallery-side wall, but it was just decorative and couldn't be used to make a cosy fire. Built-in bookcases covered the wall to the left of the fireplace all the way to the ceiling.

The skin beneath his mask was finally exposed to the stuffy, clammy air. To a man who'd been hiding his face for over ten years, the feeling of the air on his skin was liberating, but also provoked anxiety. Exposing his true face felt like dangling from a skyscraper on the end of a rope.

The face beneath the mask… He never looked at himself in a mirror. But his face, that most loathsome face, was etched into his mind. A face that had been burnt, inflamed and then burst open so that it no longer resembled that of a human being.

He painfully closed his eyes and shook his head several times. The hateful face disappeared, banished by the image of a beautiful girl. Oh, Yurie.

She alone had been his mental support for all these years. Perhaps Masaki Shingo had been right. Kiichi had only managed to find meaning in his life by keeping her imprisoned in this house, together with his collection of Issei's fantastical landscapes.

He controlled Yurie's whole life, yet she also existed in a place he could never reach.

It was fate. He knew it was fate, and yet…

She would never open her heart to him, precisely because he had kept her imprisoned for ten years. She was a doll whose spirit had been stolen from her. And as long she remained like that, he would never be able to find true peace, either.

What could he do to make her open her heart to him?

His gloved hands touched his bare chin. Even through the fabric of his gloves he could feel the rough, pitted texture of his skin.

If only his face or legs could be healed…

But hadn't he accepted his fate long ago? He did not have high expectations for the development of reconstructive surgery, and he had given up on rehabilitation for his legs very soon after the accident.

But seeing Yurie grow more beautiful each year made those crazy, hopeless feelings he thought he'd left behind long ago rear their heads again and torture him even more than before.

Kiichi was startled by the sound of a knock on the door—not either of the doors to the study but the door leading from the gallery to the sitting room. He wondered who it could be at this hour.

He quickly put his mask back on and gripped the hand rims of his wheelchair. The knock came again. A weak, timid noise almost drowned out by the storm outside.

"Who is it?" Kiichi cried out in his hoarse voice, while he wheeled himself into the sitting room and over to the gallery door.

"Who is it?" he repeated. After a second of silence, a frail voice answered.

"It's Yurie."

Kiichi immediately opened the door. His young wife was standing in the dark gallery, dressed in a white negligee.

"It's late, what's the matter?"

Kiichi was surprised by her visit. He had told her to come to his room if she didn't feel like staying alone in the tower room, but he hadn't expected her to actually do it.

"Ah, I suppose you were afraid all alone in your room."

"No."

She shook her head as she gave the unexpected reply. "That's not it…"

"But what is it then?"

Kiichi was worried now. Something was wrong. Yurie looked white as a sheet, and her lips were trembling slightly.

"What happened?"

"I heard a strange noise downstairs, so I came down from my room. The doors to the dining room were open, so naturally I was curious and went out into the gallery, then…" Yurie seemed to be struggling to find the right words. "… then I switched the light on… and I think something's happened. The back door is ajar…"

"The back door?"

"Yes. And one of the paintings in the gallery was gone."

"What!" he cried out. "Are you sure?"

Yurie shrank back, looking as if she were about to cry. "That's why I came to your room…"

"The Northern Gallery, right?"

Yurie nodded, and her husband set off in his wheelchair.

"We'll have to wake Kuramoto. You stay with me."

Just as Yurie had said, the eastern double doors of the dining room were open. Kuramoto always shut those doors before going to bed.

And again, like Yurie had told Kiichi, the back door at the western end of the Northern Gallery was ajar. It was inconceivable that Kuramoto could have missed it on his rounds.

Kiichi sent Yurie to Kuramoto's room, while he carried on down the gallery. One painting was indeed missing from the left wall, about halfway down the long gallery. The small *Fountain* had been taken, frame and all.

Kuramoto came running from the side corridor that led to his room, dressed in blue striped pyjamas.

"Sir, what's going on?"

"See for yourself," said Kiichi, pointing at the empty spot on the wall. Kuramoto cried out and rubbed his drowsy eyes.

"But… that's…"

"Somebody took the painting. That is the only possible explanation."

"The painting was definitely here when I made my rounds before going to bed."

"Then it must have happened afterwards."

The masked man gnashed his teeth and glared at his butler, who stood straight as a tree.

"You made sure to lock up everything before you went to your room, I assume?"

"Yes, I checked every door and window."

"And the back door?"

"I checked that as well, of course."

"And yet I found it unlocked just now."

"What? But that means someone has broken in."

"In this storm?" Kiichi was analysing the situation as coolly as he could. "The road has collapsed, so nobody can reach the house from town. And the lock on the back door wasn't broken. Nobody from outside could have got in unless they had inside help."

"But..." the butler began to protest.

"But the alternative is very possible. Someone from inside the house could've stolen the painting and fled through that door."

"In this storm?" Kuramoto asked, repeating his master's words. Kiichi cocked his head.

"I can't say for sure. But the fact remains that the back door was unlocked from inside the house and a painting has disappeared. The first thing to do is to summon my guests and see what they can tell me."

Kiichi ordered Kuramoto to check the doors and windows in the house again, and to make sure the rest of the collection was safe. Kiichi would take Yurie and go through to the annex.

"Mr Fujinuma, what's the matter? Oh, and you brought your wife."

The moment the two entered the annex hall, they were greeted by a charming voice. Mitamura was sitting on the sofa at the back of the room. A chessboard on a table between him and Professor Mori. Although it was already past one o'clock in the morning, the two were still playing their chess game.

Kiichi wheeled himself towards the two men, who were wearing dressing gowns and pyjamas.

"Have you been playing chess all this time?" he asked. Mitamura's eyes were bloodshot, perhaps from the alcohol or the late hour.

"Yes," he answered in a slightly nervous tone. "We're thinking of calling it a night after this game, right, Professor?"

"That's right," Mori, replied, pushing his glasses up his nose and cocking his head in puzzlement. "Is there something the matter? It's quite late…"

But Kiichi did not answer the professor's question. Instead he asked another of his own.

"Have the other guests already gone to bed?"

"Yes, ages ago," Mitamura replied.

"So both Furukawa and Masaki are upstairs?" Kiichi insisted.

"Yes. Mr Fujinuma, what's the matter?"

"Actually, a painting has gone missing from the Northern Gallery," Kiichi answered, watching the two men closely for their reactions.

"What!" came a cry from Mitamura, followed by "That can't be!" from the professor. Both men jumped up from their seats.

"How can a painting have gone missing?" Mitamura asked.

"It was removed from the wall, along with its frame. And we found the back door ajar…"

"That means—" Mori started to say, but Mitamura finished his sentence for him:

"It must have been stolen."

Professor Mori cried out that they had to call the police at once, but Mitamura reminded him that the police wouldn't be able to come because the road had collapsed.

"Oh, you're right," the professor gasped.

"Anyway, we'd better have a look ourselves," Mitamura proposed, but Kiichi cut him off and said it wasn't necessary.

"I'd appreciate it if you could call the other guests here so we can hear what they have to say."

Mori's face suddenly turned pale.

"Mr Fujinuma… I hope you don't think one of us is the thief?"

Kiichi had opened his mouth to answer the question when Kuramoto came running from the Southern Gallery. His broad chest heaved as he reported back to his master:

"There's nothing wrong elsewhere. Everything is exactly as it was when I made my last rounds."

"Thank you."

The lord of the house then asked Kuramoto to go to Ōishi's room to wake him. The butler immediately followed his master's orders. Kiichi then turned to Mitamura and Mori.

"Could I ask one of you to go upstairs to—"

"What's happening?" A voice came from the staircase hidden by the wall of the annex hall. Everyone's eyes went to the stairs.

"I woke up because of the commotion here. Mr Fujinuma, oh, Yurie is here too. What's the matter?"

Masaki Shingo came down the stairs, wearing a sweatshirt underneath a grey tracksuit. He leaned against the banister and looked around at everyone in the hall.

He covered his mouth to hide a yawn, but when Kiichi told him what had happened, his hand froze.

"Stolen?" His eyes were wide open and alert now. "But who…"

"What? One of the paintings has been stolen?!" Ōishi Genzō's loud voice blasted through the hall as he came running from the hallway. "I can't believe it! It's outrageous! How dare they!?"

"Please don't shout. You won't change anything by yelling," the masked host said calmly. Then he looked around the hall.

"Only Furukawa left, then," he muttered. "Professor, I'm terribly sorry, but could I ask you to go and wake him up?"

"Of course." The professor went up the stairs. Mitamura hurried after him, saying:

"I'd better come along too. Just to be sure."

Mitamura's words seemed to imply he thought Furukawa might actually be the thief, and that he might harm the others.

The five people remaining in the hall looked at each other with consternation as the professor and surgeon went upstairs. None of them spoke. The sound of the howling wind and the rain drumming on the roof and windows only served to make the atmosphere in the hall even tenser.

After a while, they saw Mori and Mitamura on the landing at the top of the stairs. But there was no sign of Furukawa behind them.

"What's the matter?" Kiichi asked the duo from below. "Where's Mr Furukawa?"

Mitamura leaned over the banister and said:

"He isn't there. His room is empty."

ANNEX HALL   (1:50 A.M.)

How many of those present in the hall immediately understood how mystifying the situation was?

The utter impossibility of what had happened was more than obvious to Mori and Mitamura, who had gone upstairs to find Furukawa. But the others, who had been waiting downstairs in the annex hall for their return, only seemed slightly puzzled by the disappearance of the painting and the new revelation of Furukawa's absence.

"His room is empty?" Kiichi asked again.

"Yes," Mitamura said, coming down the stairs. "His room wasn't locked and his luggage is still there."

"Perhaps he had to use the lavatory?"

"He wasn't there or in the bathroom either. We called for him several times, but he doesn't seem to be anywhere upstairs."

"But—" Kiichi began, then broke off when he realized the contradiction brought forth by this discovery. He placed his gloved hand against the cheek of his rubber mask, searching for the right words. Mitamura had stopped halfway down the stairs, looking down at his host. Mori was at the top of the stairs. His face was drained of colour. A hoarse voice eventually escaped from below the white rubber mask:

"That doesn't make any sense."

"Right," Mitamura agreed immediately. "I don't understand what's going on either."

"What's wrong? Can you explain, Mr Fujinuma? Mitamura?" Masaki interrupted in an annoyed tone. "A painting has been stolen from the gallery. And one of the guests, Furukawa, is gone too. It seems painfully obvious what has happened."

"He's right," Ōishi cried angrily. "Let's get after that scruffy rascal!"

"No, we have to remain calm." Kiichi glanced at Masaki and then Ōishi and continued: "The first problem to consider is why Furukawa isn't on the first floor."

"But it's obvious why—" Masaki began, but Kiichi cut him off.

"It's completely impossible for him not to be here."

"What do you mean?"

Seeing Masaki's puzzlement, Mitamura stepped down from the staircase.

"Our host is right, Masaki," he said. "Earlier this evening— by which I mean a few hours ago—Furukawa went upstairs to his room. After a while, you and Ōishi went back to your own rooms too, but Professor Mori and I have been playing chess in the hall here since you left. I don't usually stay up so late, but, with what happened earlier, neither of us felt much like going to bed."

"But that means…" Masaki gasped.

"You understand now, right? We've been sitting on those sofas all this time. There's no way Furukawa could've come down these stairs without us noticing."

"But…" Masaki shook his head in disbelief. "Surely you must be mistaken?"

"No, I'm willing to swear that not a single person came down these stairs," Mitamura said resolutely, but then added with a sigh: "And yet there's no sign of Furukawa upstairs."

"But that's impossible," Masaki stated.

"Exactly. The only explanation I can think of is that he's still hiding somewhere on the first floor, or that he managed to slip down some other way…"

Masaki stood with his arms folded and a frown on his face. Mitamura went past him and over to Kiichi.

"Mr Fujinuma, I think it's best if we search every nook and cranny of the hallway and all the rooms upstairs."

The masked man grunted his assent.

"I'd better join you then. Could I ask you and Masaki to carry me upstairs in my wheelchair?"

Kiichi then turned back to his pyjama-clad butler, who had been waiting for further orders.

"You stay here and watch these stairs. Don't let anyone get past, all right? Yurie, you stay here, too."

ANNEX FIRST FLOOR ~ ROOM 5 – FURUKAWA TSUNEHITO'S ROOM
(2:00 A.M.)

Masaki and Mitamura lifted Kiichi's wheelchair between them and carried it up the stairs. Ōishi followed with his unsteady gait.

Mori led the group down the hallway on the first floor. The hall lights were on; Masaki had switched them on when he came downstairs.

There was nothing out of the ordinary in the hall, which led straight to the far end of the first floor. The ceiling was high, a moss-green carpet stretched across the floor and the windows facing the courtyard had thick curtains of a matching colour.

"And you're sure he's not in his room?" Kiichi asked again. Mitamura nodded without any hesitation. A frown appeared on Mori's face as he adjusted his spectacles.

"We couldn't find any sign of him," he muttered.

"Oh, come on, this is a waste of time," Ōishi said snidely. "You're saying Furukawa just went up in smoke—that's impossible—but what if you just didn't see him coming down the stairs? What are we doing up here when we should be looking for the painting?"

Kiichi shot a piercing look at Ōishi.

"Ōishi. Would you please be quiet? I am grateful you seem to be anxious about my painting, but we need to establish what has happened first."

"But—" The dealer started to protest, but he was interrupted by Mitamura.

"Our host is right. There's no use yelling and causing a commotion now. It won't change a thing about what has already happened. You know as well as the rest of us that even if we notified the police, there's nothing they could do for us right now. Or are you suggesting we all run out into the storm to go looking for the painting?"

Ōishi puffed out his cheeks and fell silent. Kiichi addressed the other three men.

"Well then, I suppose we should check the windows in this hallway first."

The initial examination didn't take long. All the windows facing the courtyard were shut and bolted from the inside. Furthermore, they were all narrow, vertical pivot windows. No adult man would been able to squeeze through one of them.

There were two doors on the right of the hallway. The first door led to room 4, used by Masaki. The door in the back led to Furukawa Tsunehito's room 5.

Kiichi wheeled himself down the hallway, asked Masaki to open the door to room 5 and then went in. No sooner was he inside than he gave a startled grunt.

"What's all this?"

The dimly lit room was filled with white smoke and a floral scent, almost like roses. The fug was so thick that it was hard to breathe.

"It's incense," Mitamura said as he followed his host into the room. "We were surprised by it too when we came up here. I suppose Furukawa was burning incense with his door shut."

Mitamura pointed at the ashtray on the small table, where the incense had left a little pile of ash. Kiichi covered his nose, placing his hand over his mask.

"Were the lights in this room on too?" he asked the surgeon.

"No, I switched them on."

"And you also checked the lavatory and the bathroom?"

"Yes, we went inside both of them."

"I see… Masaki?"

Hearing his name, Masaki stepped into the room as well. "Yes?"

"You were in the room next door the whole time, right?"

"That's right."

"Did you hear any suspicious noises, people talking, anything like that?"

Masaki closed his eyes as if to search his memories, but then shook his head.

"No, I didn't hear a thing."

"I suggest we begin by checking everything in order," Mitamura proposed. He walked deeper into the smoke-filled room and stopped in front of the windows on the far side. He pulled the drawn moss-green curtains aside.

"As you can see, both windows are shut and bolted. Should I take a look at the windows in the lavatory and bathroom too?"

"That won't be necessary," Kiichi said. "There's ventilation in those rooms, so the windows there are fixed in place. Were the windows broken when you looked?"

"Of course not. But then I'm afraid that we are forced to accept that the impossible has occurred here. Professor, perhaps you have a theory?"

"I'm afraid not really…" Mori had been standing near the door with his handkerchief held to his face, presumably because of the smoke. "There was nothing out of the ordinary with the windows in the hallway or in this room. Mitamura and I were in the hall below from the time Furukawa went to bed to when we discovered his disappearance. The only reasonable explanation I can propose is that Furukawa is still hiding somewhere here on the first floor, but…"

Mitamura opened the built-in wardrobe before Mori could finish his sentence, but all he found inside were the clothes Furukawa was wearing when he first arrived. Then Mitamura got down on his hands and knees and looked underneath the bed. Following his example, Mori looked under the desk. But neither of them found anything.

"Oh, now you're going too far, Professor," Mitamura said with a laugh when he saw Mori peeking inside the wastepaper basket in the corner of the room.

"I thought maybe the missing painting could be hidden there," replied Mori, peering over at him through the smoke.

"Aha."

The realization that it was not only a human being they were looking for made the search more complex. Masaki and Ōishi joined in, and together they searched every nook and cranny in the room, before moving on to the bathroom and lavatory. Still they found nothing.

"How about the ceiling? Is there some way to climb up into the space up there?" Mitamura asked Kiichi, who had been silently observing the grand search. Most of the smoke had escaped through the open door, so the air in the room was less stifling now.

"I think you can climb up into the ceiling space from the hallway. I'll ask Kuramoto to take a look."

"Oh, and there's something else," Mitamura said.

"Yes?"

"Perhaps we should check Masaki's room next door too…"

"My room?" Masaki asked, surprised.

"I don't mean to imply you are hiding Furukawa, but it might have been possible for him to sneak into your room when you came down to the hall."

"Ah, yes, that's just possible," Masaki admitted.

"Let's have a look."

The five men left the door to Furukawa's room open and moved on to room 4. They were disappointed, however. They found no sign of Furukawa inside Masaki's room.

They checked the windows like they had done in room 5 and looked inside the wardrobe. They looked underneath the bed, under the desk, inside the lavatory, the bathroom… Masaki himself pulled the desk drawers out and opened his bag for everyone to see. The painting was nowhere to be found.

"The only place left is above the ceiling, then," said Mitamura, his lips twisting into a sneer. He looked down at his host in the wheelchair to see his reaction. Kiichi nodded and called Kuramoto.

He sent Masaki down to the hall to keep an eye out there while Kuramoto came up with a stepladder and a torch.

The entrance to the ceiling space was through a trap door at the far end of the hallway. Kiichi, Mitamura, Mori and Ōishi watched Kuramoto climb the ladder. He pushed the trap door up, reached through the square opening and pulled himself up.

Kuramoto spent quite some time crawling around the ceiling space above the first floor. Eventually he came back, covered in dust from head to toe. When he had caught his breath, he reported that he had found nothing.

"You're certain you checked everywhere," his master asked coldly, but the butler nodded resolutely.

"I've been up there once before, so I know my way around."

"And there was nobody up there?"

"No, sir. Not even a mouse."

Kuramoto's report made the conclusion definite: Furukawa Tsunehito had managed to vanish without a trace from the first floor of the annex. A sealed space.

DINING ROOM (8:00 P.M.)

"Yes, I agree, you could call that a perfectly sealed space," Shimada Kiyoshi mumbled, impressed. He placed the black leather notebook in which he'd been making notes on the table, together with his pen.

"Yes, it's a situation crying out for an appearance by H.M. or Doctor Fell. Although, I suppose Rawson's Merlini might be better suited to a disappearance like that."

I had already guessed that Shimada was also a great fan of mystery fiction, but some of the others seemed puzzled by the unfamiliar names. Specifically, the portly art dealer, who probably didn't do any reading at all, and the bespectacled professor, who prided himself on only being interested in his own field.

However, the surgeon, who liked to play the handsome womanizer, was looking at Shimada with an expression halfway between a frown and a faint smile. Kuramoto was standing by the wall, stony-faced as always. Yurie had looked dispirited ever since we started talking about what had happened last year, but now her face was hidden by her long hair.

Shimada Kiyoshi continued with his questions.

"Allow me to get this clear first. When you looked around the first floor of the annex, you found that all the windows were locked from the inside. Of course, none of the windows was broken either. Mitamura and Professor Mori had been sitting down in the hall ever since Kōjin went up to bed, so he should have been in his room upstairs, but he wasn't, and you couldn't find him anywhere else on the first floor either. You searched the wardrobe, looked underneath the bed and desk, even in the ceiling space. You checked everywhere a man could possibly hide. In fact, at the same time you were also looking for the missing painting, so you even searched every place a man couldn't hide, but you still found no trace of him or the painting. These facts indicate that Kōjin had indeed managed to dematerialize from the annex's first floor."

Shimada's sharp eyebrows knitted into a frown. But the tone of his voice suggested he was enjoying tackling this difficult problem.

"On the other hand, it's most definitely inconceivable, indeed, impossible for a person to actually dematerialize from a sealed space. At least, not as long as we still believe in the rules of our world—or perhaps I should say the laws of physics. You see what I mean?"

"You don't have to point that out to us a year after the fact. That's exactly the problem we've all been struggling with," Mitamura said, looking to the others for support.

"Well then, did you manage to come up with an answer?" Shimada asked. He was resting his hands on the table, twiddling his thumbs and fingers—the ones he usually used for origami. "I wasn't here that night a year ago. All I can do is look at what happened as an outsider, based on the information I've picked up here and there, and on what you have told me just now. If I trusted all the data available to me, I would also find myself forced to change my views on how this world works and what is possible in it. But you see, whenever humans are confronted with a conundrum like this, we tend to look for an acceptable

154

interpretation—one that does not destroy everything we believe in and trust to be true.

"What I would like to do now is ask about the theories each of you arrived at. Mr Fujinuma, may I ask you first? What are your thoughts on the disappearance of Kōjin?"

I removed my pipe from between my lips and answered Shimada in my hoarse voice:

"I won't pretend I've forgotten, but as I've told you again and again, I don't want to think about those events any more."

Shimada didn't seem offended and turned to Mitamura.

"What about you?"

"I have, of course, given the matter a lot of thought," the surgeon replied. "Much as you said, I assumed some sort of trick must have been used to create the illusion of an impossible disappearance, because otherwise I too would find myself forced to stop trusting the laws of physics."

"A wise conclusion."

"But what kind of trick?" Mitamura asked rhetorically as he slowly unfolded his arms. "We couldn't find him anywhere on the first floor. The only ways to leave the first floor are through the windows or down the stairs. But all the windows were locked from the inside and as far as I could tell they were of a sort that couldn't be bolted from the outside using a needle and thread, or somehow otherwise manipulated using any of the sorts of mechanical tricks you read about in mystery novels. In the end, I'm afraid I had to agree with what Ōishi said at the time. Furukawa must have managed to sneak down the stairs without Professor Mori or myself noticing." The pretentious surgeon looked somewhat humble for a change.

"Hmm, I believe the police eventually arrived at that conclusion too," said Shimada.

"I wouldn't say 'eventually'. They arrived there rather quickly as I remember," Mitamura said with a grin.

"Well, I suppose that wasn't such a surprise," muttered Shimada. "The police in our country are excellent, of course. Yes, they are very good at their job, though they do lack imagination. So, Mitamura, you admit you must have missed Kōjin coming down the stairs?"

"Reluctantly, yes," said Mitamura, scowling. "As no other possibility remains, it seems I am left with no other choice. And I should also confess I had been drinking at the time."

"Professor, do you have anything to add?" Shimada asked.

The professor looked uncomfortable as he adjusted his spectacles.

"I feel the same way. It seems the only possibility is that Furukawa did manage to get down the stairs without either of us noticing, although I still can't quite believe that's actually what happened…"

"What else could have happened!?" Ōishi cried out, rubbing his knees in frustration.

Shimada tried to calm him down.

"Now, now, let's stay focused on the crux of the problem. I made this timeline while I was listening to your accounts just now…"

Shimada stopped fidgeting with his hands and reached for the black notebook on the table.

"You've heard this all before, but allow me to read it aloud. Let's see… (These are approximate times.)

09:00 P.M. Furukawa comes down to look at paintings.
10:00 P.M. Kuramoto sees Furukawa in Northern Gallery.
10:30 P.M. Furukawa goes upstairs.

10:30 P.M. Ōishi goes to his room.

10:50 P.M. Masaki goes his to room. Mitamura, Mori remain in annex hall.

01:00 A.M. Kuramoto sees suspicious light. Yurie hears suspicious sound, goes down. Finds back door open, painting gone.

01:50 A.M. Furukawa not found upstairs.

"I hope you agree this is more or less accurate? Good. Now, the authorities would later decide that Mitamura and Mori had simply not noticed Kōjin sneaking downstairs. They concluded that he'd disappeared because he was the thief. He snuck out of his room, stole the painting and fled the house by the back door."

By this time, I was getting frustrated with his long-winded explanation.

"Shimada, we know all of that. Could you please tell us what *you* think about Furukawa's disappearance?"

"What *I* think? That's a good question. Would you accept the answer that I'm still deliberating?" Shimada said, slipping the notebook into his breast pocket. "To be completely honest, at this point I can't say anything definite. But I suppose… Yes, I'd say that the police conclusion feels off."

"It *feels* off?"

"How should I put it?" Shimada replied, a grave expression on his face. "It doesn't feel right? To use a clichéd comparison: solving a problem is a lot like solving a jigsaw puzzle. However, in this case we don't have a picture of the completed puzzle, nor do we know how many pieces there are in total. And of course, the pieces of our mystery might not be flat, but three-dimensional, or perhaps they even have four or five dimensions. So depending

157

on who is putting the pieces together, we could all end up with completely different pictures, or perhaps I should say 'shapes'.

"To put it simply, the shape put together by the police in order to explain the incidents of last year seems wrong to me. They made a mistake somewhere, and most of the pieces are in the wrong places."

"But that is only *your* impression, correct?" I pointed out.

"Mr Fujinuma is right. Why pretend there's more to what happened, simply because you feel like something is off or doesn't fit?" Ōishi said, scratching his sweaty nose. It was clear he'd had enough of the long discussion. "You're the one who says the police got it wrong, so if there's anyone here who should provide us with another explanation, it's you!"

"You're right, of course… but, hmm… I'm convinced that this intuition of mine is meaningful…" Shimada then suddenly turned to Mitamura. "For example, Mitamura has a tic of fiddling with the ring on his left hand, correct?"

"Huh?" Taken by surprise, Mitamura quickly let go of the ring he was playing with at that very moment. "I do?"

"Everyone has their mannerisms and tics. You may not be conscious of them yourself, and perhaps even the people around you may not have noticed them, but everyone has them." Shimada then looked at me. "Mr Fujinuma, for example, always extends his little and ring fingers whenever he's holding his pipe or a glass in his left hand. And the professor is forever adjusting his spectacles."

"My hearing aid is attached to the frame of my spectacles. I have to fidget to get the position of the earphone right," Mori explained, embarrassed.

"Cut it out!" Ōishi barked, gulping down his glass of scotch and water. "So what? Sure, everyone has a mannerism or two, of

158

course they do. Look at yourself, always twiddling your fingers on the table. Do you know how distracting that is?"

"Ah, so you have noticed." Shimada grinned and spread his hands open. "Does it bother you? I've been getting into origami lately, so I'm always practising all the new models I've learned with my fingers."

"Ahaha, origami?" Ōishi laughed mockingly.

"Oh, please don't underestimate origami. It's not just for children. The world of creative origami is much deeper than you'd expect. There are countless studies available on origami and… oh, I'll talk about it later.

"Anyway, please understand, I'm not criticizing your mannerisms. I just wanted to point out some examples. Suppose somebody were to stop one of their mannerisms all of a sudden. What if Ōishi, for example, stopped scratching his nose. Or it could be something even smaller. But suppose that happened. The people around you would probably sense that something was wrong, even if they didn't realize exactly what had changed. They would simply feel that something was off. That the shape in front of them was wrong somehow. That's what I mean when I say that something doesn't feel right."

"Ah. I kind of understand what you're saying," said Ōishi.

"Very well then," said Shimada, cutting the dealer off before he could say any more. He rested his hands on the table and laced his fingers together. He seemed to have made up his mind about something.

"Anyway, the puzzle feels off to me, even though I can't claim to know what the finished puzzle should actually look like. But I'm starting to have an idea where *some* pieces should go. One of them is Negishi Fumie's fall from the tower. And another piece is Kōjin's disappearance. While I haven't yet managed to tie his disappearance to the fall, an answer is slowly taking shape in my mind that feels better than the one the police came up with…"

An impressed gasp escaped from Mori's and Mitamura's mouths simultaneously. Ōishi simply huffed dismissively. He didn't look impressed.

Mitamura urged Shimada to continue. He'd started fiddling with the ring on his left hand again.

"The shape began to come together when I started to think about the architect who designed this house eleven years ago." Shimada looked at me. "What I mean is: the fact that this house was built by none other than Nakamura Seiji should have been given more consideration."

I was unable to suppress an audible gasp. The others in the room looked confused, their eyes going back and forth between Shimada and me.

At that moment, a lightning flash illuminated the view outside the windows, but Shimada kept his eyes focused firmly on my mask.

"Mr Fujinuma, once again, please forgive my rudeness, but there's one more thing I'd like to ask of you. Could you please unlock room 5 for me—the room Kōjin was staying in a year ago?"

HALLWAY ~ ROOM 5 – FURUKAWA TSUNEHITO'S ROOM   (8:45 P.M.)

Eventually I decided to grant Shimada Kiyoshi's request. Kuramoto looked after the key to that room. I had him bring it to me and ordered Yurie to stay in the dining room. I told my guests they were welcome to come along if they were interested. Mitamura got up immediately, and Mori announced he'd join us

160

as well. Finally, Ōishi also got up, though he didn't appear to be very enthusiastic.

We were making our way down the Northern Gallery on our way to the annex when Shimada spoke to me.

"Do you remember that when we first met today, I mentioned his name—Nakamura Seiji?"

"Yes, I remember."

Of course I remembered. The only reason I had changed my mind about Shimada and decided to invite the curious man into my house was because he'd mentioned that name. When he brought up Nakamura Seiji out of nowhere and said he wanted to have a look at the room in the annex, I immediately guessed what he had on his mind. This man was thinking about that *peculiar love* so characteristic of the late architect.

"You mentioned you had a curious connection with Nakamura Seiji. What did you mean by that?" I asked Shimada. I'd been wondering this the whole time.

Shimada scratched his nose, almost as if he were mimicking Ōishi.

"Are you aware that Nakamura Seiji met a horrifying end on an island in Kyūshū in September last year?" he asked.

"Yes."

I had read about it in a newspaper Kuramoto bought in town.

"It happened on the island of Tsunojima, in Beppu Prefecture, in a house he himself had built called the Blue Mansion. Seiji had a younger brother who lives in Beppu. He's a friend of mine."

"Oh."

"That is one connection. See, after the Blue Mansion went up in flames… Oh, no, let's leave it at that. That is all over and behind us. Anyway, half a year later, another horrible tragedy occurred on Tsunojima, in another strange house designed by Seiji."

"Oh, the Decagon House?"*

"Indeed. Call it fate, but I was also involved in a minor way in that incident."

"Because your brother is a police detective?" I asked.

"No, it was a private matter."

There was a brief silence. Kuramoto pushed my wheelchair down the dark hallway, as the storm raged outside. Shimada walked beside us, his eyes glazed as if he was gazing off into the distance.

"The Blue Mansion. The Decagon House. And now the Mill House. First Nakamura Seiji dies in the Blue Mansion, and then almost immediately afterwards, Kōjin gets involved with all of this... When I learned that Kōjin had disappeared, from another of Seiji's houses of all places, I felt a cold chill run down my spine."

Mitamura, who'd been walking behind us, gave a chuckle. "Surely you aren't suggesting that the architect left a curse on his houses, causing all of those tragedies?"

Shimada didn't contradict him. Instead he laughed out loud.

"That would be amazing if it were really true. It seems like we're dealing with a mystery story at first, with an honest-to-goodness impossible disappearance, and then comes the surprise twist: the real culprit turns out to be the evil spirit of the dead architect! I imagine most people would be furious if a mystery writer ever dared to try something like that. I, however, would applaud it."

"Oh, would you?" questioned Mitamura.

"I would!" laughed Shimada. "But in all seriousness," he went on, getting a hold on himself, "I don't hold with supernatural

---

* See *The Decagon House Murders* by the same author.

162

phenomena. I enjoy far-fetched ideas, but only those that remain logically plausible."

"I'm glad to hear it," the surgeon said.

"But the fact remains, three bizarre incidents have occurred in Nakamura Seiji's houses in the span of only six months. I can't help but feel that these places are home to some kind of force… And I also can't ignore the fact that I always seem to be connected to the tragedies somehow…"

We carried on through the small hall and down the Eastern Gallery. When we found ourselves in the high-ceilinged annex hall, Shimada stopped in front of the stairs, and offered to help carry me up as if it were the most natural thing in the world. He and Kuramoto lifted me between them. Mitamura had gone up the stairs ahead of us, and the three of us followed him, with Mori and Ōishi trailing behind.

Kuramoto unlocked the door, which hadn't been opened for a whole year.

"This door was unlocked when Kōjin vanished, right?" Shimada asked. Mitamura and Mori both confirmed that it was.

Kuramoto went inside and switched the lights on. The room before me merged in my mind with the scene of exactly a year ago. The lights. The drawn curtains. The bed and desk. The small table and armchair. The grey carpet covered in thick dust…

"Ah, yes, it's more or less the same as my room next door," Shimada said as he stepped into the room and looked around. "And there was incense in that ashtray?"

I nodded. Shimada then pulled out a small black case, barely larger than a sizeable pen, from the pocket of his jeans.

"Do you mind if I smoke?" he asked.

"What's that?"

"Oh, I guess this does look a little strange…"

163

He opened the case, and out came a cigarette.

"I made a promise to myself: only one cigarette a day. This cigarette case holds me to it. Do you mind?"

"No."

Shimada put the cigarette between his lips and held his special cigarette case up to the end. A little flame appeared. Apparently, the case had a built-in lighter too.

With the cigarette in his mouth, Shimada went on further into the room. He started knocking on the walls, methodically working his way over every inch. We stayed near the entrance, watching his movements.

"What are you doing?" Mitamura asked eventually.

"I'm searching," Shimada replied.

He went back over to the small table and dropped some ash in the ashtray.

Mitamura looked confused.

"Searching? For something connected to that architect, Nakamura Seiji?"

"Exactly. I'd be obliged if you could help me too."

"But—"

I decided to cut in and spare Shimada the bother of explaining.

"He thinks there might be a secret passage in the room."

"A secret passage?"

The surgeon frowned and started playing with his ring. Mori and Ōishi looked similarly unsettled. Kuramoto was the only one to seem unperturbed.

"Exactly," I confirmed. "Am I correct, Shimada?"

"Oh, yes, that's precisely what I was thinking," he agreed, visibly enjoying his one cigarette of the day.

"It seems some of you haven't heard of Nakamura Seiji's love of gimmicks. He was a peculiar man. Nobody would deny he was

164

a brilliant architect, but apparently, he never accepted requests to design normal houses. He would only work on curious houses, projects that happened to coincide with whatever theme interested him at the time, and he'd always conceal childish tricks in those houses. Of course, that's also exactly why his work attracted the attention of people from all over the world."

"And you think that there might be some of those gimmicks hidden in the Mill House?" Mitamura asked, frowning even more deeply. "But, Mr Fujinuma, if there were any gimmicks like that, you'd know about them, right?"

"No, not necessarily," Shimada said, putting out the little that remained of his cigarette in the ashtray. "Seiji would sometimes design these quirks in the houses without telling the owners. Like a naughty child playing a prank."

"But that's…"

The surgeon was taken aback by this revelation.

"And that's why it's a distinct possibility that there's some kind of architectural secret on the first floor of this annex. It could be a secret passage, or perhaps a hidden room. When I arrived, I looked around the entire first floor myself, but I couldn't find anything. So, the only place left is this room."

Shimada started knocking on the walls again. "You may have noticed that the outer walls of this building are rather thick. I suspect that if there's something hidden in this room, it's inside the wall."

But he couldn't find anything out of the ordinary. He gave a groan of disappointment and turned back to us.

"Please, don't feel you have to stay here if I'm boring you. I want to look around just a little bit longer."

"I'm out of here, then," sighed Ōishi. "I've better things to do than watch your little game."

"I'd like to help you," Mori said, stepping forward. The professor had also helped Shimada with his comment about the wet carpet, so it appeared he was feeling generous towards the uninvited guest.

Mitamura on the other hand had lost all interest the moment we started talking about secret passages. He stayed for a while watching Shimada and Mori's search with a bored look on his face, but eventually he turned around without saying a word and left the room as Ōishi had done.

I moved my wheelchair to the centre of the room, took my pipe from the pocket of my gown and placed it between my lips.

"Were you aware of any habits Nakamura Seiji might have had?" I asked Shimada, who was crawling around the floor on all fours.

"What kind of habits?"

"I mean when he created these gimmicks. Is there a common motif or pattern to them?"

Shimada cocked his head and looked up at me.

"Oh, I see. Perhaps. But I'm not really an expert on Nakamura Seiji myself, so…"

Shimada and Mori continued their search a little longer, lifting the carpet and crawling under the bed. They also searched the bathroom and lavatory, but all they found was the dust that had accumulated over the course of a year.

"That's weird…" Shimada muttered to himself disappointedly. For a while, he had looked like an innocent young boy out on a big adventure. Shimada Kiyoshi had laid out a whole line of reasoning to explain his suspicions, but in the end, perhaps even he hadn't been truly convinced there was a secret passage; he had only wished for one.

A curious house, designed by a curious architect. And an utterly impossible disappearance inside such a house.

Shimada clearly enjoyed the world of those classic mystery stories. Secret passages were another trope from that old-fashioned world, and that's why he wanted there to be one.

"It doesn't look like there's anything here," I said.

Shimada got up, brushing the dust off his clothes.

"That's weird," he muttered to himself once again. Then he turned to his search partner.

"Professor, I'm sorry for having made you waste your time and effort."

"No, don't worry," Mori said, adjusting his black spectacles. "You really awakened my curiosity too when you explained what you had in mind."

I sighed at the two of them.

"Well then, I think we've seen enough. We're not going to learn anything more about the disappearance today."

"That's weird," Shimada muttered to himself a third time. He still hadn't quite given up. "If there's no secret passage here…"

"I suppose Furukawa simply went down the stairs without Mitamura or me noticing," said Mori with an exhausted sigh.

"A very disappointing and sad conclusion it is. And yet… oh!"

Shimada suddenly ran over to the windows.

"What's the matter?" I asked.

"These windows… Would you mind if I opened them?"

"Not at all."

"These windows are the same as the ones in my room next door, right?"

"Yes. Why do you ask?"

"The windows were bolted from the inside last year," Mori put in, but Shimada shook his head.

"That's not what I was thinking about. Another theory has occurred to me …"

"Another possibility?"

"Yes, oh, but I guess it wouldn't work either."

He drew open the grey curtains, undid the latch and placed his hand on the frame of the frosted glass window. It was a pivot window, just like the ones in the hallway.

Shimada opened the window. The sound of the storm outside immediately grew louder. The wind billowed into the room with a shrill howl, making the curtains flutter crazily about.

"No, it couldn't be done here either," Shimada said with a dispirited air.

"What are you talking about?" I asked.

Shimada pointed at the open window. "This window is designed to open just a little. The gap's so tight that an adult would be hard pushed to squeeze even their head through. So I reckon the window's out of the question too. Kōjin wouldn't have been able to climb out of it whether you found it bolted or not. The same goes for the windows in the hallway."

Mori stepped towards the window himself. He peered through the open pivot. The opening was only around 15 centimetres wide.

"Could I have a look too?... Yes, it would be impossible."

"I guess in theory, you could remove the window frame and all, but these windows are built into the wall so sturdily that it just doesn't seem feasible. And then it's just a bare wall outside, nothing to climb down. And there was a storm raging outside last year, just like tonight... Mr Fujinuma, what is there below these windows outside?"

"Just some shrubs in the back garden," I replied.

"Hmm."

Shimada groaned, closed the windows again and drew the curtains. "That's ruled out too then, I guess."

"Shimada, about the other possibility you thought of…" Mori started to say as he pushed the bridge of his spectacles up his nose, but at that exact moment, lightning ran across the sky. After the white flash had faded, the room was in darkness.

The power had gone.

ANNEX HALL ~ DINING ROOM   (10:00 P.M.)

Kuramoto fetched the emergency torch he kept in the hallway, and with its help we left the room. First, we had to get downstairs.

We gave the torch to Mori, who went down first and then shone the light back up the stairs for us to follow. Shimada and Kuramoto lifted my wheelchair between them.

When we were safely on the ground floor again, Mori swept the beam of the torch around in the darkness.

"How inconvenient. Was it the lightning, do you think?" he wondered out loud.

"No, the lightning seemed to strike quite far away," Shimada answered. "I don't think it hit the house. Besides, the power is generated by the mill wheels…"

"Oh, I see. So perhaps there's something wrong with the generator, unrelated to the lighting?"

"I'll go and see at once," Kuramoto said.

"Take the torch," the professor offered.

"Thank you, but we have other torches prepared for such emergencies in the galleries."

"Let's go back to the main wing together. Yurie and the others must be worried," I said. "I wonder where Mitamura and Ōishi went off to?"

"Probably to their rooms, or perhaps to the dining room?" Mori said. At that moment, we saw a weak, swaying light coming towards us from the hallway to our left as we faced the courtyard.

"Are you all right?" It was Ōishi's voice. I could make out his portly figure behind the light. He was holding his lighter in his hand. "Oh, there you all are. Don't you have any candles around here?"

"Kuramoto?" I asked.

"Yes. In the store cupboard in the main wing," he replied.

"Let's return to the dining room first then. Shimada, I'm sorry, but if you could oblige me and push my wheelchair?"

"Good to see you're safe."

Mitamura greeted us as soon as we came into the dining room. Several candles were flickering on the dining table, around which Yurie, Tomoko and Mitamura were sitting.

"Luckily I'd just got back here when the power went out," Mitamura said, getting up and coming towards us. "I asked Ms Nozawa about candles and she managed to find some. Can anything be done about the power cut?"

"I can't tell until I've gone and taken a look in the turbine room," Kuramoto explained.

The surgeon shrugged.

"Sadly, I'm no good with machines. I don't even really know how the engine in my car works."

"I'd like to come with you, if you don't mind," Shimada said to Kuramoto as he pushed my wheelchair towards the dining table. "I've tinkered with the old generator we have at our temple a few times, so I may be able to help... Ah!"

As Shimada's cry rang out, I felt my wheelchair tilt forward. He seemed to trip and came to an abrupt stop, throwing me out of my wheelchair and onto the floor.

"Oh, no, I'm so sorry!" Shimada exclaimed, horrified.

"Are you all right?" Mitamura asked as he came running over.

There was little I could do, flat on my stomach on the floor in the darkness. I tried to worm around, conscious of the mask on my face and my legs lying stretched out on the floor, my nostrils filled with the smell of the dirty, dusty carpet—then gave up. I felt absolutely pathetic. All I could do was wait for help.

Shimada put his shoulder beneath my right arm. Mitamura grabbed me by my left hand as he helped me get up.

"Are you OK?" Shimada asked.

"Yes, I'm fine."

When I was safely back in my wheelchair at last, Shimada mumbled a shamefaced apology:

"I am so sorry. I tripped over a wrinkle in the carpet…"

"I understand. It's dark."

"Are you hurt at all?" Mitamura asked.

I told him once more that I was fine as I smoothed out my dishevelled gown. But as I peered up at the surgeon in the candlelight, the look in his eyes gave me a bad feeling.

FUJINUMA KIICHI'S SITTING ROOM   (11:00 P.M.)

Fortunately, it didn't take long for the power to be restored.

Apparently, Kuramoto and Shimada had trouble locating the problem at first because they were working in the dark, but it turned out to be just a simple fault. A loose connection somewhere. I didn't ask for details. Kuramoto told me it was Shimada who had found it. Perhaps inviting him into the house had been a wise decision after all.

We all knew that nobody would be coming out to the house to fix anything at that hour and during such a storm. If there had been a more serious problem, we would have had to spend the rest of the night with no power and only torches and candles for illumination. So everyone in the dining room let out a collective sigh of relief when the lights came on again.

After apologizing to my guests for the interruption, I said I thought it would be best if we retired for the night.

I had recently got into the habit of going up to Yurie's room and listening to a few records with her before going to bed, but that was not possible with the broken lift. I had asked Kuramoto to take a look at the lift, but he hadn't been able to do anything about it. I would have to go back to my quarters alone.

Before I left, Yurie bid everyone good night too and went up the stairs to the tower room. The look on Mitamura's face as he watched her go unsettled me. It was as if his eyes were crawling across every inch of Yurie's delicate body.

After midnight… He had asked Yurie if he could go up to her room to see the paintings there after midnight. He had also said he wanted to have a chat with her, without me knowing…

The thought of the two of them together was agony to me. So why couldn't I simply tell him to back off and leave her alone? I had a right to, after all. Every time I looked at him I could feel the anger rising in my throat, so why hadn't I said a word in the end? Perhaps because I couldn't tell what Yurie was thinking any more. She hadn't protested against Mitamura's advances in any way.

Was it because I didn't understand her? No… that wasn't it. Or perhaps…

Some kind of towering yet invisible malicious force was at work here. I tried my best to keep the ugly struggle within me a secret from the others and silently left the dining room.

I wheeled myself into my sitting room, closed the door and switched the lights on and immediately howled like a wild animal. How was it possible!? I was gripped by a terrible panic. The door in the right wall of the room—the door to the study—was open! That dark door that had been locked this whole year!

Why was it open now? I desperately tried to calm my wildly beating heart as I moved closer.

Darkness reigned in the study. The lights had not been switched on in there. I expected something to jump out from the shadows at any moment…

I slowly pushed myself into the room, peering about me, my ears pricked up for the slightest noise. It couldn't be…

Not a sound. Of course, there wouldn't be anything. And yet…

I reached for the light switch and turned it on. Finally the study's true form was revealed once more. The spines of the books lined up on the bookshelves. The darkly gleaming desk. The red brick fireplace set in the gallery-side wall.

There was not a soul inside. Everything here was as it had been. Not a single thing had changed in this sealed room.

So why was the door open? And how had it been opened? I struggled with the frenzy of questions that were overwhelming my mind.

A small black key lay on the floor. I didn't need to pick it up to realize it was the key that opened the study door.

I had to calm down. I had to think about this calmly.

The door from the gallery into my sitting room had been unlocked this whole time. Anyone could've got into my sitting room if the opportunity arose. Had someone snuck into my quarters after dinner?

But how had this key ended up here?

I switched off the lights in the study, then closed the door and locked it once more. It was an old-fashioned lock that could only be unlocked with the key, whether you were on this or the other side of the door.

I turned my back to the door which was sealed off once again and moved towards the window, fleeing from the mystery that oozed from the study. I opened the curtains a little and pushed my mask up against the cold window. Outside, drops of rain pattered on the glass. Two suspicions began to form within me. My mind kept swinging back and forth between them.

Leave. Leave this house.

The green note under my door. The threat. The open study door. The key… All these flashed through my mind.

One of my suspicions pointed me towards an unimaginable horror, towards an ominous, demented shadow lying in wait. But when I tried to flee from that dread, I ran straight into the other suspicion in my mind. Which was… No, I refused to believe it.

I stared despairingly at the stormy darkness beyond the window.

After a thorough search of the first floor of the annex, all they had managed to accomplish was to confirm that Furukawa Tsunehito had indeed vanished.

"It's just impossible," the surgeon sighed.

"Couldn't he just have come down the stairs without you two noticing?" the art dealer proposed.

"But we were sitting on those sofas, and the stairs are right there. I can't see how we could have missed him."

"But you were concentrating on your chess game, right?"

"Yes, but… Perhaps he might have been able to slip past if I were alone, but how did he manage to get by me *and* the professor? Unless he used some kind of trick."

"Masaki, are you sure you didn't hear anything suspicious when you were in your room?" Mori asked.

"I didn't hear a sound, Professor," Masaki replied.

"Don't forget it's not just that baldy priest who's disappeared. A valuable painting is missing too. We have better things to do than waste our time worrying about him," the dealer grumbled.

"But we can't just pretend he hasn't disappeared," the surgeon cut in.

"We're talking about one of Issei's most valuable works, remember?" the dealer insisted.

"I am well aware of that, but still…"

The two men began to talk over each other.

"Please calm down," Fujinuma Kiichi pleaded. "Bickering won't help at all. Now, we've inspected everything that needed to be inspected. Please let me decide what to do next."

"But we have to call the police!" Ōishi spluttered, sending out a spray of saliva along with his words.

Kiichi glared sharply at the portly art dealer.

"That is for me to decide."

"But…"

"Setting aside the problem of how he left the first floor, the circumstances do indeed suggest that Furukawa has stolen the painting. The next question is, where did he go?" the man in the wheelchair summarized.

"The back door was left open, right?" said Ōishi.

"Even supposing he did leave through that door, remember there's a storm raging outside. And he knew that the road had collapsed."

"Mr Fujinuma, you're thinking too rationally about this. You can never tell what a bloke like him will do if he's desperate."

"Excuse me, sir," Kuramoto interrupted the barking Ōishi. "Before I retired to my room, there was an incident…" He explained how he'd seen Furukawa behaving suspiciously in the Northern Gallery earlier. "He wasn't acting at all normally, sir. He almost looked as if he were… possessed."

"Hmm… Very well. Thank you, Kuramoto," Kiichi said, nodding and folding his arms.

This reminded Kiichi that he'd noticed Furukawa Tsunehito behaving somewhat strangely on occasions in the past.

Perhaps Ōishi had a point. Maybe he shouldn't expect a desperate Furukawa to have acted logically. But what should his next step be? After a moment's consideration, he said:

"At any rate, nothing is gained by making a scene now. I'll notify the police as soon as possible, but it's likely they won't be able to do anything until the road's been repaired. And I don't think it'd be wise to go outside to look for Furukawa without any idea where he's gone."

"I agree," Mitamura said. "I can't imagine he would be easy to find and I doubt he would be his usual self either. He might be dangerous."

"What about the cars? I hope they're OK," Mori said, but Mitamura didn't seem very concerned.

"I'm sure they're fine. I don't think Furukawa knows how to drive anyway."

"So we're just going to sit here twiddling our thumbs?" Ōishi complained again.

"Are you volunteering to go outside in this storm, Ōishi?" Kiichi asked, looking out through the windows at the courtyard.

"Ahem, well… I mean, no…"

Kiichi shot the stammering art dealer an icy glare, and then looked round at the rest of the guests gathered in the annex hall.

"It's my opinion that there's nothing else we can do tonight. It's very late, so please go to bed. We'll see what we can do in the morning. I trust you are all happy with that plan?"

Kiichi told Yurie to retire as well. She'd been sitting on the sofa, looking exhausted and despondent.

"Kuramoto, could you check one last time that every door and window is bolted?"

"Of course."

"Good night then," the masked host said, and turned his back on his guests.

Yurie and Kiichi left the annex together and made their way back to the main wing through the Northern Gallery. Kuramoto had gone off in the other direction to check whether the house was properly locked up as per his master's orders.

Kiichi pushed himself, while Yurie walked at his side. He noticed her delicate body trembling underneath her white negligee.

"Are you cold?" he asked in a low voice. Yurie gave a brief shake of her head, as she fiddled with the ends of her hair.

"What a night," Kiichi said with a sigh. "I'd prefer we kept quiet about it. But who could have imagined he'd pull something like this off during a storm?"

Was the man mad?

Kiichi's mind began to wander as he wheeled himself along, watching the paintings on the gallery wall go by from the corner of his eye.

Were these works so devilishly powerful that they drove men insane? It didn't seem out of the question to Kiichi. While the spell had taken a different form with him, he hadn't been able to escape the pull of Issei's art either. He lived his life more or less under the control of this collection, bound by a fixation on his father's works.

Soon he neared the back door on his right, just before the double doors to the dining room. At that moment, he heard someone approaching them from behind.

"Kiichi! I'm sorry to bother you now."

Kiichi turned around to see Masaki Shingo at the other end of the gallery, his casual outfit, a tracksuit and sweater, seeming out of place in the grand surroundings. He jogged over to Kiichi and Yurie.

178

"There's something I want to discuss with you," he said, still out of breath.

"What is it?"

The masked host sensed it was something important. He carefully studied his friend's face.

"It's about Furukawa…"

"You have something to tell me about him?"

"Yes. I didn't want to mention it just now with the others around, and also I was a bit thrown off by all the commotion, but I have an idea as to what happened…"

His eyes darted around the gallery as he lowered his voice to a whisper.

"You see, I was chatting with Furukawa earlier today—although I guess I should say yesterday now. Anyway, I got the impression that he wasn't in a very good place financially. He mentioned something about trying his hand at the stock market recently, and that it had gone badly. And I also sensed that… Yes, that the beauty of Master Issei's works had truly enchanted him, more so than anyone else. I think he must have just been overwhelmed by it all, and decided to do this terrible thing."

"Hmm."

"But supposing he did steal the painting and fled outside, I'm sure he's already regretting it."

"You are?" asked Kiichi.

"I think he must have lost his head. He just grabbed the painting and made a run for it without thinking it through. But the more he cares for that painting, the sooner he would regret running out into the storm. Imagine how he'd feel if the rain ruined it!"

"You really think that someone who'd resorted to theft would worry about that?"

"He would," Masaki said with conviction. "Which is why I believe he's still hiding nearby. He might have gone outside, but he wouldn't be able to hide in the woods. He'd need to find shelter from the rain somewhere. Like the storage shed, for example."

"Yes, you might have a point," Kiichi agreed.

Masaki looked straight into Kiichi's eyes behind his mask and pleaded with his friend:

"Could you leave this to me?"

"What do you mean?"

"Could you wait a little bit before you report the theft to the police? Let me find Mr Furukawa first. I'll try to reason with him."

"But he might be dangerous."

"I'll be fine. He's really a very timid man. He won't do anything worse than he has already."

Masaki seemed desperate to convince Kiichi. A question arose in the masked man's mind.

"Why are you going to all this trouble for him?"

"I know I'm no saint, but I can't bear to see someone like Furukawa become a criminal."

"You can't? Why not?"

Masaki sighed.

"Listen, I reckon I should come clean with you now. I wasn't planning to keep it a secret from you for ever. I hoped you of all people would understand." He grimaced, and rubbed his stubbly chin. "The real reason I'm staying at your house is because six months ago I made a terrible mistake."

"A mistake? You mean…"

Had he committed a crime?! Kiichi had had his suspicions already, but he hadn't expected to hear Masaki confess under these circumstances. Kiichi took a few deep breaths to calm himself down.

"What did you do?"

"Please don't ask. Not yet."

"And the police are looking for you now?"

"Perhaps," Masaki answered evasively. "That art dealer, Ōishi, I think he may be on to me. He tried suggesting some kind of shady deal to me earlier. But don't worry, I would never cause you any trouble."

Just then, they were interrupted by a cry:

"Ah!"

It was Yurie. She had gone on ahead and was standing at the end of the gallery, looking at the back door.

"What's the matter?" Kiichi asked, briskly wheeling himself towards her. Masaki was already at her side.

"What happened?" he asked.

"There's someone outside," the trembling Yurie explained, pointing at the small glass window in the upper half of the back door.

"What!?"

Masaki moved to the door and pushed it open, letting in a powerful gust of wind and rain. He took a step outside.

"Ah, Furukawa!" he cried, then turned to the dumbfounded Kiichi. "It's him! I saw him running away just now."

"Are you sure?"

"It has to be. I'm going after him. Please don't tell the others. I don't want to make this an even bigger deal than it already is."

"But, Masaki, you—"

"I'll be fine."

Masaki ran out into the storm, oblivious to the rain soaking him to the skin. He stopped and turned around one last time.

"This is my way of making up for what I did," he said, looking gravely at Kiichi. "Please, just go back to your room and wait for me. Yurie, you too. Please. Everything will be all right."

Kuramoto Shōji was just about to fall asleep when he heard a curious noise: a creaking, grinding, grating sound. Was it coming from outside, or perhaps somewhere deep within the house? The noise of the wind and rain was still there too, but this was completely different.

Having his rest disturbed earlier by the theft had been especially taxing for Kuramoto, who was accustomed to regular hours of sleep. Every time he tossed and turned in his bed, he felt the ache in his muscles and joints.

After his master had calmed everyone down and told them to retire for the night, Kuramoto had checked the doors and windows in the house one last time—his third round tonight. He'd found nothing amiss on this round when he ran into Kiichi, with Yurie hiding behind him, in the dining room.

The master had told Kuramoto to leave the back door unlocked. When Kuramoto asked why, he learned that Masaki Shingo had gone outside after Furukawa.

Kuramoto was shocked by the news, and suggested he should go after both of them. But he didn't feel strongly enough to insist when Kiichi said they should let Masaki do what he thought was best. Kuramoto was worried about Masaki, of course, but he was also completely exhausted. Crawling around in the ceiling space of the annex had been particularly tiring.

Then, as he was lying in bed, thinking about how his age was catching up with him, and just starting to drift off, he was disturbed by the creaking sound.

His eyes snapped open. He listened for the noise again, but it seemed to have stopped just as suddenly as it began. Had it been a dream? He shook his head and closed his eyes again.

What a day it had been, Kuramoto thought to himself, as his thoughts slowly started to melt away again.

The accident during the day, the commotion just now… There'd been strange goings-on all night. There was that light he spotted when he went to bed the first time, now that noise…

Then Kuramoto's thoughts turned to the back door, which his master had ordered him to leave unlocked.

Kiichi had told him to leave everything to Masaki Shingo, and following his master's orders was Kuramoto's job and duty. But even so… Was it really right to leave Masaki all alone outside in this storm?

He'd better not go to sleep, he decided, and reluctantly dragged his tired body out of bed. Yes, he should at least wait until he knew Masaki was safely back in the house. He'd just have a quick look. He put his slippers on, trying to shake off his drowsiness.

Kuramoto stepped out of his room and made his way through the dark side corridor and into the Northern Gallery, where he turned left to have a look at the back door. The night light set beneath the eaves outside was shining through the small window at the top of the door and illuminating that part of the gallery a little. The door had not been bolted.

Kuramoto shuffled towards the door in the dark. It was then that he noticed something wrong with the carpet.

There were black marks here and there on the scarlet carpet. These marks were wet.

Kuramoto realized immediately that they were footprints. Did that mean Masaki had returned to the house? Without switching on any lights, Kuramoto followed them past the door, and into the hallway running behind the tower.

"Masaki?" he cried out softly. Here the dim garden lights in the courtyard cast a faint glow through the windows.

"Masaki, are you back?"

No answer. All he could hear was the wind and rain outside.

Perhaps he'd gone to the master's room, to report on his pursuit of Furukawa, the butler thought.

The marks on the carpet continued at regular intervals but slowly grew fainter and fainter until they stopped at an unexpected place.

Kuramoto's eyes had adjusted to the darkness now. The footprints ended in front of the black door to the small stairwell room, which led down to the basement. The door was ajar.

The cautious butler stopped in his tracks. He was certain this door had been closed when he made his rounds just a little while earlier. Why would the footprints stop here?

He opened the door to be greeted by a raven-black darkness. He reached for the light switch and a second later, a yellow glow illuminated the landing.

Kuramoto froze in surprise.

"But that's…!"

A framed painting was lying on the floor at the top of the stairs.

He didn't even need to get closer to it to identify it. It was the painting that had disappeared from the Northern Gallery. It was *Fountain*.

But how had it got here? Had Masaki managed to find Furukawa and get the painting back? But if so why would he have left it lying here in the stairway?

Kuramoto decided he must tell his master.

He left the lights on, and softly shut the door. Then he followed the curved hallway towards the Western Gallery and his master's quarters.

"Uugh!"

Just then he was hit by a sudden, powerful blow from behind.

Kuramoto fell to his knees before collapsing on the floor. There was a blinding pain in the back of his head.

"Who—who…"

He had bitten the tip of his tongue. The nasty metallic taste of blood filled his mouth. He put his hands on the floor, to try to rise to his feet, but another blow landed on his neck.

Kuramoto lay face down on the carpet, unconscious.

FUJINUMA KIICHI'S SITTING ROOM ~ DINING ROOM (5:00 A.M.)

He blinked a few times beneath the cold rubber mask and stifled a yawn. He was leaning deep back into the wheelchair, looking across the sitting room.

He glanced up once more at the hands of the clock hanging on the wall. It was five in the morning. Less than an hour before sunrise. The storm outside was slowly starting to die down, but it was taking its time.

The thought that the storm might never leave them crossed his mind for a second.

He wondered about Yurie. He couldn't help thinking about her. She probably hadn't been able to get to sleep, all alone in the tower room. She must be lying there trembling with fear and anxiety, waiting for the day to come.

5:05 a.m. He made up his mind and left the room. The scarlet carpet in the gloomy Western Gallery looked dull grey to him. As if the darkness had robbed the carpet of its life. He felt a bead of perspiration drop down his face. He was exhausted. He had to focus or he'd collapse on the spot.

The wheelchair moved down the gallery, towards the dining room.

He switched on a single light in the dining room and slowly pushed himself over to the lift. When he stopped in front of the brown steel doors, he heard a faint noise.

"Hmmh… mmmph…"

It was a muffled voice from somewhere in the dining room.

"Kuramoto?"

The noise was coming from behind a sofa near the windows. The middle-aged butler was lying on the floor, his hands and feet bound with heavy string.

"Kuramoto, what happened?"

The butler tried to speak, but couldn't get a word out. He had been gagged. His pale, desperate face looked up at his master, pleading to be untied.

"Yes, just a second."

The masked master of the house leaned forward in his wheelchair and reached out to untie Kuramoto, frustrated by the difficulties his body gave him.

Kuramoto's hands had been tied behind his back, but the knot there had already loosened. The butler had probably been struggling to free himself for some time now. He was panting, but he somehow managed to get up onto his knees so his saviour could reach the knot better.

"Nearly there. Just a little longer…"

When his hands were finally free, Kuramoto rubbed the back of his head, undid his gag and pulled out the handkerchief that had been jammed into his mouth. He started untying his feet as he tried to explain what had happened.

"Somebody hit me from behind, sir. Out of nowhere."

"Who was it?"

"I don't know. It happened in the hallway I think. Hang on a second… Yes, that's it, the painting, the stolen painting, I found it! I was on my way to report to you when I was attacked. What time is it now?"

"It's gone five in the morning."

"And Mr Masaki?" the butler asked.

"He still hasn't come back," his master explained in his low hoarse voice. "I couldn't get to sleep myself and I was wondering how Yurie was feeling, so I decided to go up to her."

Kuramoto unfolded the handkerchief which had been stuffed in his mouth. It was a plain indigo man's cotton handkerchief.

"I know this handkerchief," the butler said.

"You do?"

"Yes. I'm sure I have seen him using it."

Kuramoto meant Furukawa Tsunehito, of course.

"I'm worried about Yurie," Kuramoto's master placed his gloved right hand on the cheek of his mask. "I'm going upstairs. You come along with me."

"Yes, sir."

Kuramoto dropped the handkerchief on the floor and got up. His head was still throbbing and he kept rubbing the spot where he had been hit.

"But sir, the painting's…"

"Yurie comes first," was the reply.

The masked master of the house turned his wheelchair back towards the lift.

TOWER ROOM   (5:20 A.M.)

Yurie was lying trembling on her large bed, wrapped in a duvet. The chandelier and wall lights had been switched off. Only the lamp on her bedside table gave off a dim light. When the two men arrived via the lift and stairs, Yurie sat up.

"Yurie, are you all right?"

She nodded. Her pale face looked on with wonder as the white mask approached her in the darkness.

"Madam," the middle-aged butler called out to her in concern. But Yurie simply covered her mouth with her trembling hands and shook her head a few times. Her long black hair swayed in the dim light.

"What's the matter?" the master of the house asked as he wheeled himself over to her bed.

"I was afraid…" She hesitated, as if looking for the right words. "I tried to get to sleep, but I couldn't. Then I saw a strange figure outside."

"A figure? What did you see exactly?"

"I don't know. It was outside that window." She was pointing to a window on the northern side of the room. "I was looking outside, when there was a lightning strike in the distance. In the light, I saw someone going towards the forest…"

"It was him!" Kuramoto said in an uncharacteristically animated manner. "He must have been running away."

"Furukawa?"

"Yes, sir. I'm sure it was him. He must have attacked me and then fled the house."

"Hmm." Kuramoto's master only grunted noncommittally in reply.

He looked up at the white-framed window and then around the room.

"Oh!"

His gaze had halted on the windows to the left of the lift, on the east wall of the room.

"What's the matter, sir?" the butler asked.

"Look!"

His master was pointing at those windows.

The curtains had not been drawn. The darkness beyond was slowly being driven away by the growing light. It was almost dawn.

"Isn't that smoke coming out of the chimney? Or am I imagining things?"

"Smoke?" Kuramoto repeated in surprise, then ran over to the window and put his face close up against it to get a better view.

There was a chimney stack on the roof, with a long, narrow flue running down the courtyard-side wall before disappearing into the ground, where it was connected to the incinerator in the basement.

"Yes, you're right, sir."

Even through the rain outside, Kuramoto could clearly make out a wisp of dark smoke rising out of the chimney and up into the sky, where it was blown away by the wind and rain. He immediately realized what this meant. Something was burning in the incinerator in the basement.

"Whatever could it be, sir?" Kuramoto looked at his master, dumbfounded. "Should I go and take a look?"

"I'll come with you. You also said you found the painting. Where is it now?"

"Oh, yes, the painting... It was lying on the floor at the top of the basement stairs."

"I don't like this," his master said. "We'd better wake everyone in the annex too. Get them at once."

"Yes, sir."

A few minutes later, they were all gathered in the hallway next to the main wing tower. The party entered the stairwell together.

The landing was dark, even though the butler was adamant he had left the lights on. Fujinuma Issei's *Fountain*, which he also claimed to have found there, was nowhere to be seen. And the stormy night was about to give way to dawn. The incidents of the night had reached their cruel, devilish conclusion. It awaited them in the darkness at the bottom of the stairs.

DINING ROOM   (12:55 A.M.)

An ear-piercing shriek rang through the house. There was no other way to describe that shrill sound.

The moment I realized it was Yurie, I flew out of my room as fast as I could and hurried down the dark Western Gallery towards the tower.

Yurie's scream seemed to go on for ever. She had probably never made so much noise in her whole life.

A faint light was coming through the gap between the dining room doors. Desperately, I pushed my wheelchair forward with all my might, practically slamming it into the doors to open them.

"Yurie!" I cried, but at the same time someone else in the hallway outside cried out in terror. I hadn't even had time to think about that cry before I heard the sound of footsteps and someone came running from the Northern Gallery.

"Sir!"

It was Kuramoto. He must have also come running from his room when he heard Yurie's cry. "Sir, it's horrible."

I turned around. His voice broke as he went on:

"It's Ms Nozawa, in the hallway."

"What's the matter with her?"

"She's lying in the hallway. I think she's…"

"What?!"

Just then I noticed a white figure from the corner of my eye.

"Yurie."

She was standing at the top of the stairs in her white silk negligee.

"Madam," Kuramoto called out to her.

It was clear the butler didn't know what to do first: deal with the matter of Nozawa Tomoko in the hallway, or check that Yurie was OK.

The main lights in the dining room were off. The room was only dimly illuminated by the wall lights. I looked up at Yurie and called to her.

"Yurie, was that you screaming?"

She gave no reaction whatsoever, just leaned dumbly against the banister with her eyes staring into the distance. Then she started slowly coming down the stairs.

"Madam, is something the matter?"

Kuramoto had noticed something was wrong with Yurie and rushed to meet her on the stairs. At that moment, someone came running into the dining room from the direction of the Northern Gallery.

"What happened?"

It was Shimada Kiyoshi, wearing black jeans and a T-shirt. Judging from his clothes, he hadn't gone to bed yet. When he saw me, he said:

"I heard that scream all the way over in the annex. Was it—"

He broke off as he noticed Yurie coming down the stairs.

"I was right. It was. What happened?"

I wheeled myself over to him.

"Shimada. It seems Tomoko is lying in the hallway outside."

"Tomoko? Oh, your housekeeper!"

Shimada seemed stunned.

"That's horrible. Where exactly?"

"Next to the windows looking out into the courtyard," Kuramoto explained.

Shimada immediately left the room. For a moment I wondered whether it was wise to let him go off on his own, but I was worried about Yurie. She had finally made it down the stairs and was leaning trembling against the wall, her eyes darting anxiously about the room. Her beautiful face had turned pale as a ghost. Her colourless lips quivered and her eyes were filled with tears.

"What happened?" Kuramoto asked her again, but she didn't say a word, only weakly shook her head.

"Yurie," I said, and was about to move towards her when Shimada Kiyoshi came running back, out of breath.

"Mr Fujinuma, Ms Nozawa... She's dead! I think she's been strangled. She's been murdered!"

A strangled gasp escaped from Yurie's throat. She clapped her hands to her ears and slowly collapsed down the wall to the floor.

"We have to call the police at once. Where's the phone?" Shimada said, alarmed.

"O-over there," Kuramoto stammered.

"You'd better call the police then while I wake the others," Shimada said quickly and ran out of the room once more.

Kuramoto went over to the telephone table, while I moved to Yurie's side. She was sitting at the bottom of the stairs with her back to the wall.

"Oh, Yurie..."

She didn't look me in the eye, even though she must have realized I was right next to her. She still looked completely dazed, her teary eyes darting about frantically. Her long hair was clinging to her cheeks and neck. Her trembling lips kept opening slightly and closing again, as if she was trying but failing to tell me something.

"You have to get a hold of yourself. Tell me what happened," I said sternly, trying to get through to her, but she still couldn't utter a single word. All I could do was watch her in silence as I struggled to remain calm myself.

"Sir?" Kuramoto had finished his call to the police. He was still holding the receiver in his hand. "They're coming at once. I was told not to touch anything at the scene, or the body, for any reason."

"How long will it take for them to get here?"

"The officers from the station in A— will set off at once. But with the storm it will probably take them close to two hours, assuming there aren't any problems with the road. It'll take even longer for the additional forces from the Prefectural Police to make it here."

There was a heavy feeling in my chest. In my mind's eye I pictured the poor housekeeper's contorted face and gasped in sympathy.

Shimada came back a few minutes later, followed by Mori Shigehiko and Ōishi Genzō. They were both dressed in their pyjamas, so they had probably been asleep, and were out of breath after hurrying over from the annex.

"It's strange, I can't seem to find Mitamura anywhere," Shimada said, coming over to me.

"Really?"

"No. He didn't answer the door, so I tried opening it. Turns out he hadn't locked his room, but there wasn't a soul inside. I even checked the bathroom and lavatory. Nothing. How about the police? Have you called them already?"

I nodded. "But it will take a while for them arrive. We'll have to be patient."

"I can't believe this," Ōishi barked with a scowl on his face. "Is this really happening all over again? What's going on in this house?"

"I wonder where he could've gone? I sure hope he's all right," said Professor Mori with a grave expression on his face.

"Aaaah! Aaaaaaah!"

All of a sudden, a series of panicked cries echoed through the high-ceilinged room.

"Yurie?"

"Madam?"

Everyone was startled. Yurie had started to scream.

"Nooooo! Uuuuuh…"

There was terrible fear in her wide-open eyes. Her lips trembled horribly as she slowly lifted her delicate hand. It appeared she was finally coming back to her senses.

"What is it? What's happened?" Shimada crouched down at her side. "Try to calm down now. Can you tell us why you screamed?"

"R-r-room."

She had finally uttered a word.

"Room? Which room?"

"My… my room…"

Her raised hand was now pointing to the top of the stairs.

"All right, your room. Up in the tower."

Shimada jumped to his feet again, ran over to the stairs and flew up them with the speed of a sprinter.

We all looked on astonished as Shimada disappeared up the staircase. Immediately after there came a cry of concern.

"What's the matter?" Professor Mori called out, starting to climb the stairs too.

There was no reply. A tense silence took hold as we waited, frozen. The professor stopped halfway up the stairs awaiting an answer.

Eventually, Shimada's slender figure appeared on the landing. "It's terrible. Mitamura is dead."

TOWER ROOM   (1:45 A.M.)

I instructed Kuramoto to take care of Yurie while Mori and Ōishi carried me up the stairs. The lift was still out of operation.

Mitamura Noriyuki's dead body was behind the grand piano in the centre of the tower room. He was sitting on the piano stool, his back to us, wearing dark-blue trousers and a caramel-coloured long-sleeved shirt. His upper body was slumped forward, his face resting on the lid. Just as Shimada had told us, the surgeon would never move of his own accord again. He'd been reduced to a mere object.

"The back of his head has been smashed in," Shimada explained. He was looking at Mori and Ōishi. The direct confrontation with such a visceral sight had rendered them speechless. Shimada was also looking at me, but he could not read my reaction beneath my white rubber mask.

"He was murdered, that's clear as day."

Shimada looked pale as a sheet and his voice was trembling. He'd been playing the detective all this time, but I sensed that tonight was the first time this man had actually seen the body of a murder victim.

Not that I was in any position to criticize. Even after the horrifying experience of a year ago, I still couldn't suppress the chill that surged through my body.

"That is probably what did it," Mori said, timidly pointing to something lying at the corpse's feet. A black nail puller, approximately thirty centimetres long, lay on the floor.

"Agreed," Shimada said. He crouched down and examined the tool. "There's blood and hair on it. Mr Fujinuma, do you recognize it?"

"I can't be sure."

"Where do you keep your toolbox?"

"I think it's in the store cupboard."

"All right."

Next, Shimada brought his face closer to the back of Mitamura's fractured skull.

"The wound looks fresh. The blood hasn't dried yet."

"But why was he up here in the first place?" said Mori, taking a step forward. His fingers were resting on the frame of his spectacles.

"Shouldn't we get out of here? It's a crime scene," grunted Ōishi, scratching his nose. "The police will know what to do."

"Yes, you're right, of course. But still…" Shimada slunk swiftly over to the other side of the piano. "Mitamura has been murdered, and downstairs Ms Nozawa was strangled to death. So, someone in this house has killed two people in a short period. It will take some time for the police to get here. We can't be sure we're safe until they arrive."

"But… you can't mean…" the art dealer stammered.

"Do you mean the murderer is one of us?" Mori's clichéd question was met by Shimada with a grave frown.

"It is possible. Of course, I can't deny the possibility it is somebody from outside the house."

"In any case, we should leave this room," I said. "I can't bear being in here with his body any more."

"Yes, of course," agreed Shimada.

He turned to go back to the stairs again, but then stopped short.

"Oh, no, wa-wait just a second," he muttered, as if hit by a sudden realization.

"What is it now?"

"Look at this," Shimada said, pointing to Mitamura's hand. "Don't you think that's odd?"

Urged on by Shimada, we timidly approached the corpse. The surgeon's upper body was resting on the piano lid. His right arm was crooked above his head, and he was clutching his left hand in his right.

"A rather strange position to die in," Shimada mused, looking down at the body. "If you look closer, you'll see his right hand is holding a finger on his left hand. This might have been his last deliberate action."

"Deliberate?" I asked. Shimada nodded back at me with a solemn expression.

"Yes. What I mean is, isn't this a dying message?"

"A dying message?" Ōishi cocked his chubby head. Mori seemed equally puzzled.

"A clue left to us in his dying moments," I whispered, examining the body's positioning.

"Exactly. What if Mitamura knew he wasn't going to survive the attack, but wanted to tell us who his killer was?" Shimada explained.

"Aha. But what could he be getting at with this pose?" Ōishi asked with a frown.

"Perhaps he's pointing to his ring?" Mori suggested.

"His ring?"

"Yes, take a closer look. His right hand is holding on to the ring finger on his left hand. Doesn't it look like he was trying to pull his ring off?"

"Hmm," Shimada grunted. "It's hard to imagine he'd start

fiddling with his ring in his final moments. Oh, that reminds me. Last year, the victim's finger was missing a ring, wasn't it?"

"Yes," the professor said.

"Oh, I've got it!" Ōishi suddenly cried out.

"What is it?" Shimada asked.

"He's trying to take his ring off. He's trying to tell us that the person who killed him was the same person who killed Masaki last year and stole his ring."

"What?!" protested Mori plaintively.

"You mean, Furukawa Kōjin has come back?" muttered Shimada. "And that he's murdering people this year, too? That's what you're implying, right?"

"I just can't believe that…" said Mori, pushing his spectacles back up his nose.

Ōishi seemed frustrated and scratched his nose again. "You haven't forgotten the horrible things he did last year, have you?"

"The suggestion is worth considering. It's possible the killer came from outside the house. But still…" Shimada stepped away from the body. "First, let's get out of this room. And, Mr Fujinuma, it might be wise to ask Kuramoto to check the doors and windows one more time."

DINING ROOM (2:15 A.M.)

"… I was taking a shower. I always do that before going to bed. But when I got out of the bathroom, Mitamura was lying there on the piano…"

Yurie was calmer now after drinking a little brandy. She was lying on a sofa in the dining room, slowly explaining what had happened.

"How long were you in the bathroom?"

"About thirty minutes."

"And you're sure there was nobody in your room when you went into the bathroom?"

Yurie fell quiet for a moment after Shimada Kiyoshi's gentle question, but then slowly nodded.

"Do you know why he had come up to your room?"

"No."

Yurie looked down at the floor. I noticed that she was blushing slightly.

She was lying. She had known he was going to visit her in her room. But... I couldn't reveal this to everyone else. How could I?

I needed to talk to her alone. If I could just ask her how she really felt...

"Did you hear anything while you were in the bathroom?" Shimada continued.

"... No."

"When you got out and discovered the body, did you notice anyone else in your room?"

"... No."

Shimada was sitting on a sofa opposite Yurie. Professor Mori was sitting next to him, shoulders hunched. Ōishi was at the dining table, sipping from the whisky he'd taken from the sideboard.

Just then Kuramoto returned, having finished his rounds of the house.

"Did you find anything?" Shimada asked, getting up from the sofa.

"The back door was open," Kuramoto reported in a grave tone.

"I knew it!" Ōishi rasped, before draining his glass. "It's that crazy priest again!"

"Ōishi, please calm down," said Shimada sharply. "It's too soon to jump to such conclusions. Kuramoto, are you sure everything was locked when you went to bed?"

"Of course. I checked all the doors and windows as I do every night."

"And there was nothing amiss with the paintings in the galleries?"

"No."

"And the paintings in the archive?"

"No problems there. That room is always locked securely."

"Hmm… So the back door was open. Had the lock been broken from the outside?"

"No, the lock is intact."

"Aha. That means that if the murderer *is* someone from outside, they must have snuck into the house before you carried out your check. Either that, or they had help from someone inside."

"Someone inside?" Ōishi got up from the dining table and joined the others by the sofa. He scowled at Shimada. "If that's true, I reckon you are the most likely suspect."

Shimada stared up at Ōishi, dumbfounded. He looked as if he had been confronted with a solution in a detective novel—one he found completely outrageous.

"I am?"

"Who else would it be!?" Ōishi spat out. "You're friends with that priest. You could have planned it all beforehand. Then you turn up here, out of nowhere, and somehow manage to trick Mr Fujinuma, worming your way into the house…"

"Surely you must be joking," Shimada said, spreading his arms wide theatrically. "For what? To kill Mitamura and Ms Nozawa? Because I'm some crazed murderer?"

"The paintings, of course. You're working together to steal Issei's paintings. And you killed those two because you got caught."

"So we got caught stealing the paintings, and then I went all the way to Yurie's room to kill Mitamura? That doesn't make any sense. Professor, do you mind if I ask you what you think?"

"Sorry, I have nothing to add."

Mori had crossed his arms, as if he was hugging himself. He was hunched over even more than before.

"Mr Fujinuma, then?" Shimada looked at me. I'd been sitting in my wheelchair, next to the sofa side table. I looked back at him through my cold mask, and answered in a cautionary tone:

"I can't deny that Ōishi's theory has, to a degree, aroused my interest. We don't know you at all, so it's only natural for us to be suspicious."

"But if you consider things calmly…"

"You should be aware that it will be difficult for anyone to think calmly in a situation like this," I fired back.

I looked at Yurie. She had curled up on the sofa.

"Look, she's frightened. I don't know when the police will get here, but Yurie and I will go back to my quarters for now."

"But, Mr Fujinuma—" Shimada began, but I cut him off.

"I am the master of this house. Even in these circumstances, in fact exactly *because* we're in these circumstances, I must ask you to comply with my wishes. Yurie, come with me."

Yurie got unsteadily to her feet. It was as if her body had been drained of all energy.

But Shimada still wouldn't give up.

"Please wait, Mr Fujinuma. It's slowly becoming clear to me now. I can almost see it. The shape that fits perfectly."

"The police will solve these murders. I've had enough. I hope you aren't suggesting I am the murderer?"

With these final angry words, I pushed my wheelchair towards the Western Gallery. Yurie followed me with an unsteady gait.

The fierce storm was still raging outside. On my back I could feel the puzzled gazes of the group in the dining room. Inwardly I cursed not the storm outside, but the one inside, the storm that was about to rage through the house and complete the wreckage of our peace.

INTERMISSION

Memory

The stormy night would soon give way to dawn. A thick bank of clouds slowly parted. Mountain tops covered in a pale mist pierced the eastern sky. While the rumbling of thunder and the heavy rain had passed, the fierce wind showed no sign of relenting. The trees in the forest still creaked as they swayed in the wind, the river was high and the three massive mill wheels kept on turning next to the manor hidden deep in the valley.

The six of us went down into the large, bleak basement.

The lantern-like lamps flickered weakly on the bare concrete walls. A washing machine, dryer and a basket full of clothes stood against the wall near the bottom of the stairs. Several ducts crawled along the ceiling.

I pushed myself forward before coming to a halt and folding my gloved hands on my stomach. I was wearing a brown nightshirt, too large for my slim frame. Yurie stood close behind the wheelchair. Ōishi Genzō and Mitamura Noriyuki had positioned themselves on either side of her, as if to protect her. Mori Shigehiko was hanging back a bit, perhaps because he was afraid. Kuramoto stood impassively at his side.

"Could one of you…" I croaked. "Could one of you open that incinerator door?" A slight tremor could be heard in my voice. It was probably the tension. I was sweating under my white rubber mask.

Ōishi stepped forward. He went over to the incinerator and picked up a black bar lying on the floor. A steel poker.

"Aaah!"

He let out a muffled cry just as he threw the poker away and fell backwards onto the floor.

"What is it, Ōishi?" I asked.

"It… it's…"

The art dealer was sitting on the floor, pointing towards where he had dropped the poker.

Yurie let out a shriek. I turned around to her.

"Yurie, don't look."

"Come on," said Mitamura as he put his arm around her shoulder and turned her away. Yurie nodded weakly, a terrified look on her face, and walked unsteadily back towards the stairs. Mori and Kuramoto moved in front of Yurie, forming a wall to block her view.

The surgeon swiftly walked over to Ōishi still sitting on the floor, and looked down at him.

"What is it, Mitamura?" I asked.

"It's exactly what it looks like, sir," Mitamura replied calmly. "A human finger. Looks like the middle or ring finger."

I pushed myself over to look for myself. It was ghastly pale, like a dead caterpillar. At one end was an ugly stump covered in dried blood.

"The cut appears to be quite fresh. This finger was probably cut off less than two hours ago," Mitamura said.

"But… what…?"

"That's the question."

Mitamura crouched to get a closer look at the finger lying on the floor.

"Aha… there's a pretty deep indentation here. A mark left by a ring."

"Ah."

I put my fingers through the eyeholes of the white mask on my face, placing them on my closed eyelids.

"It has to be Masaki's."

"I'm afraid I must agree," Mitamura replied, standing up once more. The fingers on his right hand started playing with the gold ring on his left ring finger. "I assume it's the mark left by Masaki's cat's eye ring…"

"So he must have murdered Masaki…"

"That I can't say at the moment."

Ōishi finally managed to get up from the floor.

"Mr Fujinuma, does this mean that inside the incinerator…" he asked, but I shook my head ambiguously.

"Could you open the door?"

"But… err…"

Ōishi's cheeks trembled and he looked like he was about to fall over again. Mitamura shrugged and picked up the poker instead.

"I'll do it," he declared as he stepped towards the incinerator. It was a medium-sized incinerator for household garbage, a tarnished silver in colour, set on a concrete base. There was a chimney pipe at the top, right at his eye level, going straight up to the ceiling of the basement room where it disappeared and led outside and all the way up to the chimney Kuramoto and I had seen smoke coming out of earlier.

We could hear the crackling of a low fire from inside the metal container. No one, of course, would be burning waste this early in the morning. So why was it lit?

The poker in Mitamura's hand approached the hot door. A metallic clank echoed through the room as he hooked the end of the poker through the handle.

The door swung open. The fire was blazing inside.

"Uugh."

We all covered our noses as a sharp, pungent smell wafted out of the incinerator. I can't have been the only one who gagged.

It was the smell of burning meat. But what made the smell especially horrifying was that we all knew what was really burning.

"Masaki…" I called out mournfully.

"I can't believe this…"

Mitamura stuck the poker in the incinerator. Several blackened objects lay in the fire on top of each other.

He searched the incinerator. He seemed calm, except for the fact that the hand holding the poker was shaking slightly. Eventually he stuck the poker into one of the burning objects and tried to pull it out.

"Waaah!"

He jumped back. As he was pulling the object out, he had inadvertently brought something else with it, which fell onto the floor.

Several loud cries reverberated around the basement.

Mitamura let out a desolate wail as he stared at the round object that was now lying on the floor.

"How horrible…" he whispered.

It was a decapitated human head, burnt black and still smoking. All the hair had been burnt off and the eyes, nose and lips rendered unrecognizable by the blazing heat.

The poker in Mitamura's hand was still sticking into the other burnt object.

"This must be an arm then," he whispered as he threw it into an empty metal bucket nearby, eager to be done with it.

It was indeed an arm.

Like the head on the floor, the arm had been blackened and contorted by the heat. It appeared to be a left arm. But what attracted their attention was the hand: it was missing one finger. The fourth finger counting from the thumb: the left ring finger.

This was the burnt dead body of a human being.

One body, which had been cut up in six parts, not counting the finger: head, torso, two arms and two legs.

Thus the nightmare of that night ended, and the storm slowly receded. After the clouds had cleared, the sun appeared as if nothing had happened. A morning began, just like any other...

But the dead did not begin their lives anew, and the missing left only a great mystery behind.

We were exhausted and confused, waiting for the police who would hopefully solve the case. When the experts finally arrived in the early evening of the 29th of September, they were all stunned. Relentless questioning, an examination of the crime scene and a search of the vicinity soon followed.

Eventually the "incidents" of that night would be buried underneath the "solution" to which their investigation had led them. Peace returned to the valley, and I hoped with all of my heart that this peace would last.

OFFICIAL FINDINGS REGARDING THE MURDER AT
FUJINUMA KIICHI'S RESIDENCE—THE MILL HOUSE

*Time period: 28th September (Saturday)–29th September
(Sunday) 1985.*

*(Excerpts from the notes of Shimada Kiyoshi.
Based on police reports, newspaper, magazine articles, etc.)*

1. *Findings regarding the body.*
   *The following facts were learned from the examination
   and post-mortem of the body found on the morning of*

29th September in the basement of the Fujinuma Kiichi residence.

A. The body had been cut into six parts: head (1), torso (1), arms (2) [*left ring finger had been cut off], legs (2). These parts had been burnt in the incinerator in the basement.

B. Identification was made difficult due to the heavy damage the body had sustained, leading to the loss of recognizable physical characteristics such as facial features. The victim was male, age 35–45. Height approx. 165 cm, average build, slightly underweight. Albuminoid degeneration caused by the heat made it impossible to determine the blood type of the victim.

C. Cause of death: asphyxiation. Strangulation by hand or via an instrument: both are likely. It was impossible to determine the time of death because the fire had led to an advanced process of carbonization in the body.

2. *Identification of the victim.*

A. The victim was determined to be Masaki Shingo (age 38) based on the testimonies of the people involved regarding the events of the night, the police examination and the post-mortem examination, as well as the physical evidence found in the basement. The victim Masaki Shingo had been living in the Fujinuma residence.

B. The physical evidence used for identification as mentioned in 2A was the left ring finger found on the floor next to the incinerator. This finger corresponds with the missing finger on the left hand of the victim. It is assumed the culprit accidentally dropped the finger on the floor when putting the body parts into the incinerator. Forensics confirms that the ring finger matches the known blood type of Masaki Shingo (O, Rh positive).

c. The ring finger had an indentation left by a ring. This tallies with the fact that Masaki Shingo wore a ring on that finger. The fingerprint of the finger also matches the fingerprints found in the room Masaki used and on the keys of the piano on which he had played.

3. *Timeline of the murder.*
The culprit of this crime is assumed to be Furukawa Tsunehito (age 37) based on various facts. Furukawa had been a guest in the Fujinuma residence since the day before the body was discovered. The following is a reconstruction of the crime based on the evidence uncovered.

A. Furukawa Tsunehito is registered as a resident of Takamatsu City, Kagawa Prefecture. Occupation: deputy priest of — Temple in Takamatsu City. Like the three other guests at the Fujinuma residence at the time of the incident, Furukawa was an obsessive fan of Fujinuma Issei's works in the collection owned by Fujinuma Kiichi. He had shown signs that he was very troubled by his lack of financial means to buy a painting. Later it was discovered that he had recently tried his hand at the stock market without the knowledge of his family. His failure had put him in a very precarious financial situation.

B. Furukawa's obsession with Issei's work drove him to the theft of one of the paintings hanging in the galleries of the Fujinuma residence. The theft is assumed to be a crime committed on the spur of the moment and not premeditated. The butler, Kuramoto Shōji, witnessed Furukawa acting unusually around that specific painting on the night of the crime. This testimony further confirms Furukawa's unstable state of mind.

C. Furukawa waited until most of the household had gone to sleep before he left his bedroom on the first floor of the annex, where the other guests were also staying. He managed to sneak unseen past Mitamura Noriyuki and Mori Shigehiko, who were still awake and sitting in the annex hall. Furukawa then stole the painting and fled through the back door, but did not get far due to the storm.

D. Masaki Shingo saw Furukawa outside and chased after him. Furukawa killed his pursuer (Masaki).

E. The following explanation can be proposed for Furukawa cutting Masaki's body into pieces and putting them in the incinerator. It is likely he wanted to destroy the evidence that a murder had been committed in the first place. There is no murder without a corpse. That is why Furukawa came up with the idea of burning the body in the incinerator in the basement. The body was cut into smaller pieces so it would fit inside. If the people in the house had not noticed the smoke and discovered the body burning in the incinerator, it is likely Furukawa would have returned to the basement when the body had been reduced to ashes in order to retrieve the remains and get rid of them.

F. The instruments used to cut the body up were a meat cleaver and hatchet, which had been taken from the kitchen and the store cupboard. These instruments had also been placed inside the incinerator. It is assumed that the dissection was done outside the house, but the exact location could not be found. It is likely the rain destroyed all traces.

G. On his way to move the body parts to the basement to burn them, Furukawa ran into the butler, Kuramoto. He knocked Kuramoto out and left him tied up in the dining room.

H. The finger was cut off because while dismembering the body Furukawa wanted to steal the valuable cat's eye ring that Masaki wore. The ring was stuck on Masaki's finger and could not be removed without cutting off the whole finger.

I. When Furukawa realized the others had gone down to the incinerator, he gave up on the idea of disposing of the remains and fled with the stolen painting. It is unknown where he fled to, but due to the collapsed road, it is probable he went into the mountains.

4. *Addendum*
   Subsequent investigation resulted in the discovery of the following facts.

A. The victim Masaki Shingo had been the main suspect in a robbery and attempted murder case that occurred in February 1985 in the Nerima Ward of Tōkyō. Masaki had been borrowing money from individuals involved in organized crime for several years, due to personal circumstances. It is suspected he committed the crime because he was having trouble paying his debts. The authorities had been searching for Masaki, whose whereabouts had been unknown for six months. He had not been officially deemed a wanted suspect at the time due to the lack of conclusive evidence.

B. Soon after the murder at the Fujinuma residence, Furukawa Tsunehito was placed on the wanted list. His whereabouts, however, remain unknown to this day.

FUJINUMA KIICHI'S QUARTERS   (2:40 A.M.)

As soon as we were back in my sitting room, I locked the door to the gallery from the inside. Yurie's head was still hanging despondently and she didn't say a word. I checked that the door to the study was still locked as I wheeled myself over to it and then I had her open the door to my bedroom.

"You come in too," I said to Yurie, who was standing still in the doorway. She entered the dark bedroom, swaying as she moved. She reminded me of a sleepwalker.

A flash of lightning lit up the closed curtains of the courtyard-facing windows. One second, two seconds, three seconds… I counted the time between lightning and thunder as I moved myself over onto the bed. I switched on the nightstand light. The moment it illuminated the room, the sky rumbled. The thunder was far away.

"Come over. You can sit here."

Following my orders, Yurie sat down on the edge of my bed. She kept her head down, not once looking me in the face—my white mask.

"Are you feeling better now? Can we have a quiet talk?"

I tried to speak calmly while I suppressed the many emotions whirling within me—confusion, anxiety, agitation and anger.

"What I want to ask you first is… that man… Mitamura. Why was he in your room? Did you know he was coming up there?"

Yurie shook her head.

"You didn't know?"

"… No."

She had said the word very faintly, but I heard it clearly. She had wilfully lied to me. I didn't know what to think. After all that had happened, why was she trying to keep secrets from me?

"You shouldn't lie to me," I said finally, with an aching heart. "You knew he was coming, Yurie."

She didn't reply. She was sitting with her knees together, her small hands resting on top of them. Her hunched shoulders shuddered.

"Why won't you tell me the truth? Why are you doing this?"

Still she said nothing.

"Won't you give me an answer?"

I decided to say it. I looked straight at her head still hanging down.

"I know. I overheard you talking to that man in the small hall before dinner."

Yurie shuddered again. She raised her face slightly. Terrified eyes looked at me from behind the veil of her hair.

"He told you he'd come to your room after midnight tonight. And you agreed."

Perhaps Yurie had already realized I knew about their secret meeting. She looked back at the floor again. The hands resting in her lap were shaking.

"I was waiting for you to tell me. I wanted to believe in you. And yet…"

I broke off. Then I raised my gloved hands and reached behind the mask sticking to the skin of my face. I untied the string holding the rubber mask in place and slowly lifted it off. In the gloomy darkness, I revealed my accursed face.

215

"Yurie." Never before had my voice sounded so cold when calling out her name. "Look up. Look at my face."

But she still didn't look up.

"Mitamura went to your room like he told you he would, didn't he? That was before you went to the bathroom. You waited for him to come before you went to take a shower, didn't you?"

No response.

"Did you want to sleep with him?"

Still, she was silent.

There was another flash outside, followed after a while by a clap of thunder. It was almost as if the weather was mocking our melodrama. Yurie's silence was driving me to distraction, yet I also managed to find some sympathy for her, somewhere deep in my heart. I tightly squeezed the mask I had removed from my face.

"Yurie, I have to ask you this now. What are your true feelings for me? Perhaps I've misunderstood you all this time. I simply don't know you any more."

I placed my rubber face, still warm from my body heat, on the side table and pulled the threatening note from the pocket of my gown.

"You know what this is, don't you?"

I tossed the folded paper towards Yurie's lap. Her hands flew up and reached out for it, but the note didn't even reach her and instead fell weakly on the floor with a faint noise. Yurie didn't pick it up.

"Tell me. Why did you write it?"

I knew it; I'd known it for a while. The note had already been slipped under my door when we passed through the Western Gallery yesterday to greet the three men. But I simply hadn't seen it then. That was all there was to it.

216

No, actually, I probably had *seen* the so-called stain on the carpet Shimada had mentioned, but pathetic as I was, I hadn't realized it was the note.

Yurie, on the other hand, could not have overlooked it. That was what convinced me: the author of that note had been none other than her.

"And you were also the one who unlocked the door to the study," I continued. "Why did you do it? Were you trying to scare me? Why!?"

I had been wavering between two hypotheses since discovering that the sealed door to the study had been unlocked. One of them was that Yurie had opened the door.

I had lied to Shimada Kiyoshi when I told him the key to the study had been lost. The key was actually kept in the drawer of a cabinet in my bedroom. There was no other key. I later confirmed that the key I found lying on the floor was indeed my own key—the one that had been in the drawer.

The simple conclusion was that Yurie had been the one to open the door. She and I were the only ones who knew where that key was.

And while I knew all of this, deep in my mind I had wanted to pretend it wasn't true.

But Yurie being the "culprit" would explain the childishness of both these acts. Yurie has lived more than half of her life in this house, in the tower room, cut off from most information in the outside world. She wouldn't have any idea how to truly frighten someone. Every socialized human learns the basic means of threatening someone from the flood of books, television dramas, and crime reporting that overwhelms each and every one of us. But for Yurie, who wasn't even allowed to watch television until last year, figuring out that she needed to disguise her handwriting when writing the note was the most she could manage.

She kept her silence, so I pleaded with her again.

"Please tell me, Yurie." I could feel the emotion in my voice and had to suppress it. "Why did you try to frighten me like that? Telling me to leave the house. That's what you wrote. Is that really what you want?"

"… No."

Finally, she had answered me.

"No?" I repeated. "What do you mean?"

"… I want to leave this house. I want to go away. And that's why…"

I didn't know what to say.

Yurie fell silent again. I couldn't find the right words either. Confused, I tried to understand what she meant.

Yurie wanted to leave… Of course, this wasn't a surprise.

I loved her, and all I wanted was to live a peaceful life together with the one I loved. I always believed she felt the same way. Actually, no, even I am not that conceited. In truth I was always afraid deep down… Afraid of a future when she would turn towards the outside world and leave me, abandoning me here in this valley.

Maybe Yurie had sensed this fear of mine. She knew very well that even if she had confided to me that she wanted to go, I wouldn't have let her. I would never let her go. And that's why she tried to threaten me from the shadows, to get me to leave this place… Perhaps so that she could leave with me?

Yes, it was easy to imagine how things could have gone. I felt I was finally beginning to understand what Yurie been trying to achieve with the note. But at the same time the more I thought about Yurie, the less I understood about her as a person. I used to think I knew her, but now her heart had moved away beyond my reach.

I was speechless. I picked up the mask from the nightstand, stuffed it in the pocket of my gown and left Yurie—her head still hanging—alone in my bedroom.

FUJINUMA KIICHI'S SITTING ROOM (3:00 A.M.)

I wheeled myself over to the window and stared out into the darkness. My unmasked face was reflected faintly in the glass.

How hideous I am, I thought. I wasn't always this way. I used to have a sharp spark, some glint in my eyes. But now they were empty, like the scared eyes of an animal...

My thoughts turned to Yurie's slumped figure in the bedroom. She had come up with those silly threats, all simply so she could escape this house. She wasn't a girl any more. She had wanted to betray me as a woman, as my wife—to betray her own husband. She'd been held captive in this strange hideaway out of time and space for so long... That was the reason for her bewitching beauty, but it was also why she could be so foolish...

What was she thinking of now, in that undeveloped mind of hers, now that our peace was slipping away from us? What would happen to her after all this was over?

I had clung so desperately to my cherished peace. But then all of us must die one day, so perhaps our peace wasn't supposed to last for ever either... And perhaps I had already sensed, long ago, this day of destruction approaching.

What would happen to her, to me and to the Mill House? I could torture myself thinking about it, but it was all too late now.

219

Too late? No... I tried to push the thought away. There was still one ray of hope.

I stuck my hand in the pocket of my gown, groped around for my mask and put it back on my face. I couldn't give up now. Determined, I turned my wheelchair and pushed myself towards the door to the gallery.

There was still something I could do.

But just at that moment, I heard an unusual noise. What was it? There it was again.

It was a quiet sound, but so unusual that it stood out. It sounded like the creaking or grinding of metal...

As I listened, the creaking noise seemed to synchronize with the sound of the mill wheels revolving on the other side of the Western Gallery. While the noise was faint, it persistently reverberated throughout the room.

Then I realized. I had heard this sound before. But when, and where?

That was it! I remembered almost immediately. It was on that night! I had heard the same noise on that night! The same infernal creaking that I was hearing right now!

Where was it coming from? I listened carefully, hoping to trace its source, but I soon arrived at an unbelievable conclusion.

It couldn't be... Could the sound really be coming from the other side of the locked study door?

After a moment, the noise stopped. I tensed up in my wheelchair. All of my senses were focused on the dark mahogany door.

What had happened? What was going to happen? My nerves got the better of me and I trembled as a horrifying thought crossed my mind.

I was sweating all over, clenching my teeth so tightly that it hurt. I concentrated on the door, waiting for what I knew was going to happen. No! Nothing would happen, it was impossible!

I heard a faint shuffling noise. This was different from the metallic creaking. It was the sound of someone moving about deliberately.

There was another shuffling noise, followed by the rustling of clothes. And then came the sound of footsteps. Somebody was carefully walking across the carpet on the other side of the door!

But it couldn't be! A horrible fear gripped me as my suspicions grew darker and darker. I couldn't believe what I was hearing!

There was somebody walking around in the locked study at that very moment. But that was impossible. Who? Why? How did they get in there?

All these questions reverberated around in my mind, destroying every bit of the logic and common sense I was trying to hold on to. Despite myself, I was led to one inevitable conclusion.

The footsteps were coming towards the door now. I heard someone take hold of the knob and begin to turn it. I felt I was standing on the very brink of reality, a chasm opening at my feet. I finally lost control.

"Go away!!" I cried out in a frenzy. "Return to where you came from!! And don't come back!!"

Yurie cried out from the bedroom too. She must have been horrified by the sounds behind the door and frightened by what might be coming.

I heard him try to turn the knob once more. When he realized the door was locked, he knocked.

"Stop!!" I covered my ears over my mask and cried out like a madman. "Please, I beg of you. Don't come any closer!"

It had to be him. It had to be the man who had vanished into thin air exactly a year ago. Yurie hadn't written that note or opened the study door after all. It had been that man all this time. He'd been roaming the house, tormenting me.

My nerves gave way completely then. My mind was a blank, and all I could do was cry out at the top of my lungs, begging him to leave us alone. Eventually I started to sob as I pleaded with him.

I didn't know whether he had heard me. The knocking on the door stopped. Outside the rain kept falling, but inside, an empty silence suddenly fell.

All at once I felt drained, and sank deep into my wheelchair.

"Sir?" Someone called out to me from behind the door to the gallery. It was Kuramoto. He'd heard my cries.

"Mr Fujinuma?"

"Sir, are you all right?"

The other guests who'd stayed in the dining room must be with him too.

"What's the matter, sir?" Kuramoto insisted.

"Oh…" I began, glancing over at the door to the gallery. It was still locked from the inside. "It's nothing," I concluded eventually.

"But, sir, you…"

"It's really nothing."

At that moment, I heard another creak coming from the bedroom. What was that? It sounded like a door opening. Was it the connecting door between the study and the bedroom?

Yurie! Had she taken the key from the cabinet drawer and opened the door?

"Ah!"

Yurie let out a soft cry. Then I heard those footsteps again, but they weren't coming from the study. They were coming from inside my bedroom. The ghost inside the study had finally managed to escape through the door Yurie had opened for him!

The footsteps came closer and I saw the knob of my bedroom door slowly turn. It was only at this moment I finally realized how foolish my own imagination had been.

Footsteps? But that would be impossible.

"Who's there?" Kuramoto and the others were still in the gallery, but I couldn't resist the urge to cry out the question: "Who's there?!"

The doorknob stopped turning. The door opened...

"Oh, boy, that was close."

Out of the darkened bedroom stepped a lean man with an apologetic smile on his swarthy face: Shimada Kiyoshi!

"I was getting afraid I would need to go all the way back again. Thankfully, Yurie was kind enough to open the door for me."

FUJINUMA KIICHI'S SITTING ROOM   (3:30 A.M.)

I sat dumbfounded in my chair as Shimada walked past me towards the gallery door. His grey shirt was filthy and he trailed a nasty smell through the room.

Shimada unlocked the door and let the men into the sitting room.

"Shimada? Where did you come from?" the merchant cried out in surprise.

Ōishi, Mori and Kuramoto all came inside. I sat with my back turned to them and didn't say a word.

"Gentlemen, I finally know what our puzzle looks like. Yes," Shimada said in a clear voice, "the completed shape is essentially how I had imagined it. It is truly a crime beyond belief."

"What do you mean?"

"What I mean, Ōishi, is that I have got hold of the truth."

223

Shimada left the three men and came over to me. He coughed, covering his mouth.

"Excuse me, it's all this dust." He looked down at me. "Did I startle you?"

"W-What? Well, I mean…" I stammered.

I could feel the gazes of the three men behind us burning on my back. Eventually I got a hold on myself.

"I think you are the one who should explain himself, actually, Shimada. And depending on your answer, I may have to take measures…"

Shimada frowned and softly clicked his tongue.

"Sir, the time has come to give up."

I was dumbfounded once more.

"You planned and executed a spine-chilling crime. To preserve your dignity, you should at least behave graciously as the curtain falls."

I couldn't suppress the tremor in my voice as I cried: "You… You dare accuse me of being a criminal?"

"Would I be wrong?"

"This is outrageous. What crime do you claim I have committed?"

"All of them," Shimada answered without a second's hesitation. "You killed Mitamura. And after that, Ms Nozawa happened to witness you as you made your way back to your rooms, so you killed her too."

"Nonsense!"

"And that's not all. You're also responsible for everything that happened last year," Shimada continued. "You pushed Negishi Fumie from the tower balcony. You are of course the one who stole the painting, and you are the person who left that dismembered body burning in the incinerator."

"Shimada, wait," interrupted Mori. "That's simply inconceivable."

"Exactly," Ōishi agreed. "One of us could, maybe, but Mr Fujinuma of all people could never have done all that."

"You are completely right, yes." Shimada nodded a few times while he brushed the dust off his shirt. "It would have been impossible for Fujinuma Kiichi. He had a solid alibi when Negishi Fumie fell from the balcony. As for the body in the incinerator, he wouldn't have been physically able to go down the stairs to the basement by himself due to his disability. Similarly, he wouldn't have been able to murder Mitamura tonight. Because the lift is broken, Fujinuma Kiichi couldn't have gone up to the tower room. Yes, it would have been utterly impossible for him."

"Have you gone mad?" I mustered all the spirit I still had and glared at the man standing in front of me. "I never should have invited you to my house."

"Indeed, it was a mistake," Shimada said with a grin. Then he seemed to examine me more closely. "Well, perhaps it's not as simple as that. Even if I hadn't come along, perhaps fate would still have brought about your downfall sooner or later."

"Fate?"

"Yes. The fate of Nakamura Seiji's houses and those who live in them."

I threw my hands up in the air.

"Stop it," I begged. "Leave me alone. Everyone, get out."

"I'm sorry, but I can't," Shimada said.

He moved slowly closer. I backed away, but he kept coming, looking down at me with pity, as if I were a wounded animal.

"Do you really want me to pull that mask off your face, Mr Masaki Shingo?"

Yurie let out a short cry. She must have been listening to us from the neighbouring bedroom.

Shimada glanced over at the bedroom door, then turned back to me.

"Are you worried about her?" he asked me. "Should we call her in?"

"No… Don't."

I shook my head weakly.

"Masaki, perhaps I am just imagining things, but I suspect that the threatening note I found yesterday in front of this room was written by her."

Shimada had called me by *that name* without hesitation. I gave no answer, and he responded with a satisfied nod.

"I knew it. 'Leave. Leave this house.' She was trying to intimidate you by making it appear as if somebody in this house had learned of your crimes—not only yours, but hers too. She probably hoped you would take her with you when you left."

I still gave no answer, so he went on.

"Yesterday evening, you gave the matter of exactly when the note had been slipped under your door a lot of thought. When I later surmised that Yurie could have written the note, it suggested you hadn't noticed the note lying under the door as you passed down the gallery, but when I thought about how easily I had seen it, it was hard to imagine how you could've missed it, especially considering the low line of sight from your wheelchair.

"But the truth is that the note *was* there, and you really *didn't* notice it. A green sheet of letter paper lying on a red carpet. Normally it would stick out like a sore thumb. But not to you, right?"

"Ah…"

A low groan escaped my lips. He was right. I hadn't noticed the note. No, I *couldn't* have noticed the note.

"You lost your fiancée in the car accident caused by Fujinuma Kiichi twelve, no, thirteen years ago now. Kiichi's face and limbs were badly injured, but miraculously you came out almost unscathed. I say 'almost', because the accident did in fact lead to a serious physical complication for you, Masaki, and because of it you, an artist with a bright future ahead of him, had to give up the paintbrush.

"Mitamura knew about it. I asked him a few questions to see how much he knew. He told me about an extremely rare case, where brain damage can also affect colour vision. The accident caused severe colour blindness, very similar to red-green colour blindness. That's what happened to you, right?"

"Yes," I groaned once more.

Indeed, my eyes had been so affected that it had been impossible for me to continue my career as an artist. I had been robbed of the colours I had known my entire life.

Red-green colour blindness is usually hereditary, and most sufferers still perceive the two separate colours up to a degree, even if they're very hard to distinguish. Apparently, it's common for people to not even realize they have red-green blindness until it shows up in a test. My case, however, is different.

All shades of red and green lost their colour after my accident. They all appeared the same to me. A dull grey filter had been placed over my eyes.

My future with my beloved, and my future as an artist. All I held dear in life had been stolen from me in that one cruel moment. How I suffered, how I cried. And how I cursed that accident—and Fujinuma Kiichi, who'd been driving the car…

227

That's why I didn't notice the sheet of paper slipped under my door even though my eyes had superficially registered it.

The faded scarlet carpet in the main wing, the moss-green carpets and curtains in the annex, they all look the same grey to me. The green mountains surrounding the house, the shrubs outside, all are drab and colourless. When Shimada arrived at the house yesterday, I found it very hard to make out his red car parked among the colourful foliage of the densely packed trees.

"Shimada, what do you mean?" asked Mori, interrupting my thoughts. "How could Mr Fujinuma be Masaki Shingo? Masaki was murdered last year."

He and Ōishi had come further into the room and were standing near the sofa.

"What I mean is that the body you discovered in the basement last year did not belong to Masaki Shingo. You of all people know very well that the body had been burnt beyond recognition in the incinerator, and that it was impossible to identify it. It was a corpse the culprit had prepared as a replacement for himself."

"But they checked his fingerprints."

"Yes, or rather they checked his fingerprint," said Shimada, raising his hand. "They only checked the print of his ring finger that was lying on the floor."

"Ah!"

Mori finally realized how the trick had been pulled off. Ōishi and Kuramoto also seemed to grasp what Shimada meant.

"That ring finger alone did truly belong to Masaki Shingo, and it hadn't been cut off by the presumed killer, Kōjin, in order to steal the ring. The finger had been left there by Masaki himself in order to make everyone think that the body in the incinerator was his own."

Shimada looked at me again.

"You know, I had a strange feeling about you all along. Do you remember when at dinner, I pointed out that curious habit of yours? Whenever you hold your pipe or a glass in your left hand, you always extend your two outer fingers: your ring and little fingers."

He made a fist with his left hand, and then extended his ring and pinkie fingers. His little finger was completely straight, but his ring finger could not be extended as far.

"You often see people extending their little finger like this, but it's actually pretty difficult to lift the ring and little fingers together. It didn't look natural to me, and so that's why I started to wonder what exactly was inside your glove.

"Professor, Ōishi. Do you recall how we discovered Mitamura's body in the tower room? Yes, I mean the posture of the body—which I proposed might have been a dying clue.

"Mitamura was lying on the piano, holding his left ring finger with his right hand. Ōishi suggested he was trying to remove his ring. But that wasn't the message. It wasn't about the ring. He was indicating the finger itself. He wanted to tell us who had killed him by drawing our attention to his left ring finger."

"But why was he killed in the first place?" Mori asked.

"Professor, remember when I accidentally threw our host out of his wheelchair during the power cut? I think that's when it happened. Mitamura helped him up again, holding him by his left hand. The feeling of the hand must have made him suspicious. Anything to add, Masaki?"

I was silent.

Shimada was right again. Mitamura had grasped my left hand and looked suspiciously at me. I knew right away that his intuition meant trouble. I feared he'd noticed I was missing my left ring finger.

"That is why you decided to kill Mitamura. But I don't know why you decided to commit the murder in Yurie's room."

I bit my lip in silence. Yes, that was also a mystery to them. It was what I had seen through the keyhole of the door of the tower room that made me decide to murder Mitamura Noriyuki there.

I couldn't sit still knowing that womanizer was going to visit Yurie's room in the middle of the night.

Fujinuma Kiichi had been restricted to his wheelchair for many years, and since the lift was out of operation, he would not have been able to go up to the tower room. His was the mask I wore, but as long as no one saw me, I could walk up and down the stairs as I pleased.

When the time came, I quietly left my room, hid in my wheelchair behind the dining room door and waited for Mitamura. I didn't have to wait long. He was patting his hair into place as he quickly disappeared up the stairs to the tower room.

I got out of my wheelchair, followed him up the stairs and lingered outside the room, trying to hear what was going on inside.

For some time Mitamura did as he'd told Yurie he would: he admired the paintings in the tower room and discussed them with her. But after a while his voice took on a seductive tone. He began to praise her beauty and shower her with flattering words. Eventually I heard the rustle of clothes and a low sigh.

"… Please stop…"

It was Yurie. But despite what she later said, she did not ultimately reject the man's advances.

"Please don't say that. Yurie, you know I…"

"… We can't."

"Don't you like me?"

The clichéd lines eventually came to an end.

"… I'm going to take a shower," Yurie said, embarrassed.

"OK, I'll be waiting for you when you get out, princess," Mitamura said happily.

I clenched the nail puller I had brought with me in my gloved right hand. I saw red. I had planned to kill Mitamura after he left the tower room on his way back to the annex, but the desire surging within me wouldn't allow me to wait a second longer.

When I saw through the keyhole that he had gone to the piano and had his back to me, I quietly opened the door and snuck into the room. He was probably imagining what he was going to do with Yurie as he sat on the piano stool and waited.

When I had finished, I quickly left the room and went back down the stairs. I had committed this murder without making a thorough plan as to what I would do afterwards. I thought if I unlocked the back door, it would suggest the possibility that someone from outside had entered the house. I ran from the dining room to the Northern Gallery, and that's when I bumped into that woman, Nozawa Tomoko, who had just come out of the lavatory.

She probably never realized exactly what was going on. How could she? All of sudden she was confronted with a wheelchair-bound man sprinting down the gallery.

It was almost sad to see her so confused. An instinctive fear made her turn and run, but I managed to tackle her from behind and strangled her with my bare hands. She died without even making a sound.

I desperately tried to calm my raging nerves while I made my way back to my own quarters and waited for Yurie's scream, which I knew would come.

Shimada had also correctly guessed how I came to kill Nozawa Tomoko. He carried on:

"Just now after you had gone back to your rooms, I decided to have another look at Ms Nozawa's body. I was careful not to disturb the crime scene, but examined her neck—the strangulation marks left by the fingers are still visible, and I was able to make out that the murderer's left hand was missing a finger."

Disguising my face behind a mask, concealing the slight difference in build between me and Kiichi with a loose-fitting dressing gown, always speaking in a hoarse voice, never letting myself be seen out of my wheelchair, wearing gloves to hide my hands and always filling the empty left ring finger with stuffing... For the last year I had been leading a peaceful life, playing the role of the masked master of the house. I had always been extremely careful, especially around Kuramoto. And of course, I also had to be cautious in front of the guests. But I simply hadn't had the time to even think about the marks I'd left on Nozawa Tomoko's neck.

When I finally saw my mistake and at the same time realized the meaning of the message left by Mitamura, I had to face the fact that my cunning plan was starting to fall apart.

"Did you unlock the back door to make it seem like the murder had been committed by an intruder? Perhaps you hoped to make it look like the work of Furukawa Kōjin, just like last year. Or were you simply planning to kill all of us one by one as we figured it out, and then put the blame on Kōjin? I can't even imagine what you had in mind."

I closed my eyes, listening to Shimada's clear voice. Ōishi's rasping tones suddenly interrupted him.

"But, Shimada, listen, it still doesn't make any sense to me. Can't you explain everything so that I can understand?"

"Yes, of course," Shimada said.

But then he paused for a moment. I could feel his eyes on me.

232

"Well then, it's a role that doesn't really fit me, but allow me to explain in simple terms the logical process that led me to the truth.

"To be honest, I had no idea at first. I only sensed a vague shadow hiding in the darkness, the obscure contours of the shape I was looking for. Perhaps it was just a feeling, as Kōjin's friend, that first convinced me he would never have killed anyone. But even from an objective point of view, it was clear that the official police 'solution' to the incidents of last year, had been nothing more than a contrived explanation based solely on superficial facts.

"After I arrived here yesterday and discussed what had happened last year with all of you, I became convinced that Negishi Fumie's fatal fall was not an accident, but that she had been pushed. The only people who could have done so were Mitamura, Professor Mori, Ōishi and Masaki. The timing would have allowed Kuramoto to do it too. That would have meant that he was lying about seeing her fall past the window in the dining room, of course. The others—Mr Fujinuma, Yurie and Kōjin—all had alibis, so they could not have been involved.

"Then I started thinking: assuming Negishi Fumie was murdered, why was it necessary for the murderer to kill her?

"I have to admit I was at a loss for an answer to this question. The known facts on their own did not provide any motive for her murder. That was the first wall I ran into.

"Then I proceeded to my next problem: the disappearance of Furukawa Kōjin. How did he manage to escape the first floor of the annex?

"The police concluded that the men in the annex hall—Mitamura and Professor Mori—must have failed to notice Kōjin coming downstairs. That seemed like a hasty conclusion to me.

233

My suspicions only increased after hearing your detailed accounts myself.

"The first instinct I had was that there might be a secret passage somewhere on the first floor of the annex. The notion of secret passages is a big cliché in mystery novels, but I thought I'd give it a try—and as you know, there wasn't one. Thus I found another gigantic wall blocking my path. Oh, by the way, Professor…"

"Yes?"

"Do you remember I mentioned something about another possibility when we were searching room 5 in the annex?"

"Oh, yes, I remember, you mentioned it just before the power cut."

"Indeed. What I meant was the possibility that Masaki Shingo had helped Kōjin get out of the first floor of the annex, since he too had been there at that time. Kōjin could've climbed out one of the windows, after which Masaki could have bolted it from the inside.

"But my idea was immediately shot down when I discovered that the windows in that room don't open far enough for a human being to pass through. The windows in the lavatory and bathroom don't open at all, and the windows in the hallway are the same as in the room. Even ignoring the matter of the bolt, no adult could get out through those windows. It's impossible.

"You could consider the first floor a perfectly sealed space, then. And yet someone did indeed vanish from there. Unless we plump for the cheap solution that Mitamura and the professor both failed to notice Kōjin, we are forced to change our minds about everything we assume to be true of the laws of physics.

"But I think the person who was shocked the most by this impossible situation was Masaki himself. All you wanted was to make it appear that Kōjin had disappeared under *suspicious* circumstances. You only wanted everyone to believe he had stolen a painting and run off. You hadn't expected the surgeon and professor to still be in the annex hall at that hour.

"It's simple once you know the answer, but it had me puzzled for a long time. Ultimately, it turned out that to solve this problem it was necessary to resist the lure of the easy answer: that the two men had failed to notice Kōjin. It was only by going further, by accepting the impossible situation and treating it as such that I could inevitably connect it to the singular truth. And in the end the answer was ridiculously simple."

Shimada paused for a few seconds, like a teacher waiting for questions. He looked at Mori, Ōishi and Kuramoto, one after the other.

"The professor and Mitamura didn't fail to notice Kōjin sneaking down the stairs. There was no secret passage. And yet a person disappeared. And by that I mean that a human being physically left that space. Ignoring the stairs, the only way to get from our sealed space—that is, the first floor—was via the windows. But it was impossible for anyone to get out through them.

"Here it became necessary for me to apply logic more strictly. It was impossible for anyone to have left through the windows. However, when I said 'anyone', I really should have said 'anyone living'. It was impossible for anyone living to get out through the windows.

"But wouldn't it have been possible for someone to leave through the window if they were dead, and cut up into pieces? Let me put it differently. If Furukawa Kōjin truly managed to vanish from the first floor, the only way he could have done it was as a dead body cut up into smaller parts."

Mori and Ōishi gasped. But Shimada had more to add.

"The possibility that Kōjin could have passed by unseen, combined with the assumption that he was the culprit, made this obvious answer invisible to everyone. Of course, Masaki and Yurie 'witnessing' Kōjin alive later on worked as the perfect screen to keep it hidden.

"Furukawa Kōjin was already dead when he disappeared from the first floor of the annex. He had been cut into pieces and smuggled out through the window. When you look back at the incidents last year with this theory in mind, all the pieces come together to form a clear shape.

"And if Kōjin was murdered on the first floor of the annex and cut into pieces there, only one person could have done it: Masaki Shingo. And that means that the cut-up body found later that night did not belong to Masaki Shingo, but to Kōjin. At this stage, it is easy to imagine how the body was swapped.

"That night Masaki Shingo killed Kōjin after he returned to room 5. He undressed him, carried him to the bathroom and, using the meat cleaver and hatchet he had got ready beforehand, he cut the body into six parts. He probably put each piece in a black plastic bag and threw them outside the house through the window. I assume the weapons and clothes were disposed of in the same manner. He burned all that incense in order to mask the smell of blood in the room. And after Kōjin had been spirited away, Masaki used a lighter or torch to signal to his accomplice waiting in the tower room, to let her know the deed had been done."

"Accomplice? You mean, Yurie too?…" Mori exclaimed, adjusting his spectacles once.

"Yes, she is the only person who could be Masaki's accomplice. The suspicious light Kuramoto happened to see from his room was Masaki signalling to her."

The horrifying images from that night flashed through my mind again. Furukawa Tsunehito's pale face when I went up to his room around eleven o'clock. The depression written on his features, so pained was he by the thought that he lacked the financial means to ever obtain his beloved paintings. I got him to let me in, making out that I was going to cheer him up, but then at the first opportunity I got behind him and slipped a rope around his neck. He was dead before he knew it.

Afterwards, I took a deep breath, locked the door of the room and proceeded with my next task. I had to cut the body up into pieces in order to burn it in the incinerator later. Also, Furukawa had to disappear from the house in order for him to be suspected of the theft. Even if the plan had only been to hide his body in the basement, carrying him around the house like that would have been far too risky.

First, I undressed him. I put his clothes in one of the black plastic bags I had brought with me. Then I undressed as well (so I could wash the blood off myself later) and carried the body to the bathroom. I didn't use the bathtub, because I feared the blood would coagulate and stick to it. I left the shower running and cut the flesh under it with the meat cleaver, using the hatchet to get through the exposed bones.

Grey blood spattered around, covering my body. The stench made me sick. It took me a good ninety minutes to finish cutting up the body.

I put each part in a different bag and threw them through the window outside into the darkness. I thought this would be safe, because it was raining heavily and I also knew that the room directly below belonged to Professor Mori. If he were sleeping, not wearing his spectacles and hearing aid, he probably wouldn't hear them hitting the ground. Even if someone happened to look outside, it was unlikely they could make out the black plastic bags in the darkness.

Next, I meticulously cleaned the bathroom of the blood and bits of flesh, washed my own body and put my clothes back on. I happened to see a box of incense lying on the desk, so I decided to use it to mask the smell of blood in the room. Otherwise, I would have broken a bottle of cologne in the sink or something similar.

Finally, suppressing the urge to throw up, I snuck back outside into the dark hallway, and used a torch to signal to Yurie in the tower room.

"When Yurie got the signal, she came down from the tower and removed the painting from the Northern Gallery wall. I assume she then hid it in the stairwell landing. The theft of the painting had to take place after Kōjin's death, in case anyone noticed it was missing before he had 'disappeared'. Then she unlocked the back door to suggest someone had left the house, before going to Kiichi's room to inform him of the theft.

"That's how the commotion about the stolen painting started. Then you all learned about the disappearance of Furukawa Kōjin, and eventually the jigsaw puzzle pieces were put together in the wrong shape.

"Masaki knew that Kiichi wouldn't want to contact the police. He also knew that the road had collapsed from your call with the police earlier that evening. If that hadn't been the case, I assume he would have cut the phone line himself in order to delay the police's arrival. He also counted on the fact that Kiichi, who felt responsible for the pain he had caused Masaki, would indeed let him deal with the matter if Masaki asked him.

"Yurie lied about having seen someone outside the back door and Masaki went out chasing after the imaginary Kōjin. He told Kiichi to wait in his room while he ran out into the rain, then made his way to the exterior walls of the annex, where he retrieved the plastic bags he had thrown in the shrubs and brought them to the back entrance.

"And so he carried Kōjin's dismembered body down to the basement to burn in the incinerator, but what would he do after he had made the body look like his own? In reality it wouldn't just be Kōjin who had disappeared but Masaki Shingo too. So where would he go?

"At this point it was extremely easy to connect the missing Masaki Shingo with the current Fujinuma Kiichi. A mask, gloves, a wheelchair, a hoarse voice, his physique, a 'wife' as his accomplice… Fujinuma Kiichi had already furnished all the necessary elements for an identity swap."

Shimada turned back to me. I hadn't said a word.

"I honestly couldn't believe it at first. Having committed an irreversible crime, you then planned to erase your own existence, in order to get your hands on everything: Yurie as your beautiful wife, this house, its wealth and Issei's paintings. Your goal was to eliminate Masaki Shingo entirely and to be reborn again as Fujinuma Kiichi. I assume your wish for revenge on him, responsible for placing you on this path towards self-destruction, was part of your motivation too.

"I guessed you and Yurie got involved—as lovers—after you came here in April last year, seeking help from Kiichi. You came up with this plan when you realized she would help you.

"You carefully observed Kiichi's appearance and his daily life. He always wore a mask in public, hardly saw anyone and never left the house. Your physical builds were pretty similar too. So

239

that's when you started thinking about whether you could kill him and take his place.

"You carefully studied Kiichi's style of speech and his habits. You concluded that it would definitely be possible for you to pass for him as long as you could mimic those characteristics. However, you had two major obstacles. And one of them was Negishi Fumie.

"She was responsible for taking care of Kiichi. She helped him bathe, cut his hair and even monitored his health. It would have been impossible to deceive her. That is why you had to kill her. Once she was dead, you could ask Yurie to take care of you. The only person you had to be careful with then was Kuramoto, but you judged that you could fool him with your acting. Masaki, any objections so far?"

He was right. I knew I could fool the guests who only visited once a year with the mask, gloves and gown, and by mimicking Kiichi's hoarse voice. I also judged that I could fool Kuramoto, who doesn't pay all that much attention anyway—he serves the Mill House itself not its master. I just had to be careful not to speak to him too much. There was only one obstacle. That busy-body housekeeper.

When Negishi Fumie came up to the tower room to tidy up, Yurie told the housekeeper that she had a message for her from Masaki; that he wanted her to wait for him in the tower room because he had to discuss something with her. Yurie and I had agreed on this story in advance.

Fumie was quite fond of me, because we used to discuss Yurie's education from time to time. She trusted Yurie, so after she had finished cleaning, she waited for me in the tower room.

After making sure Kuramoto had gone from the annex to the

kitchen in the main wing, I snuck into the dining room and went up to the tower. I decided to use the lift, because I was afraid Kuramoto might leave the kitchen and come over to the dining room any second and I wanted to be out of sight as quickly as possible.

Fumie seemed puzzled to see me coming up in the lift, but didn't suspect a thing. We talked for a few moments, until eventually she turned her back to me. I took that chance to hit her on her head and knock her out. Then I dragged her out onto the balcony and threw her over the edge. I had loosened the bolts of the railing beforehand to make it seem like an accident.

The second before I threw her over, however, she regained consciousness and started to scream. She was still screaming as she plunged head first into the canal below.

From the stairway landing, I could hear Kuramoto flying out of the dining room, after which I too sprinted downstairs. I made sure to push the call button of the lift to bring the cage down again before leaving for the Northern Gallery.

I was worried about my wet clothes, but I had no time to change them. I ran back to the annex as fast as I could. From there I followed the others who had been drawn to the entrance hall by the commotion.

"The other problem you faced was the question of how to erase Masaki Shingo from the face of the earth.

"When a swap occurs in a mystery story, it's usually between two people: the victim and the culprit. But in this case, it would have been very difficult to use Kiichi's body as a replacement for Masaki Shingo's, even if you cut the body up and burned it in the incinerator. There was too great a risk of discovery because of the damage done to Kiichi in the car accident: the injuries to his face, arms and legs would have given the game away immediately.

"And there was the matter of blood type, too. I assume your blood types aren't the same. The high temperature inside the incinerator would make a blood test impossible. However, there was a risk that the body would be discovered early and salvaged before the proteins had been wholly destroyed by the fire.

"You therefore realized that you'd need a third body to solve this conundrum. Yurie had told you about the guests who visited every year. You started to look for the one who was the best match for you in terms of age, physique and blood type. And that person was Furukawa Kōjin. Maybe Yurie knew his blood type already, or maybe you made sure of it yourself while chatting with him. In any case, both you and Kōjin turned out to have blood type O.

"So, you decided to murder Kōjin and pass off his body as your own while simultaneously setting him up as the murderer and making it seem like he was on the run.

"Let's go back to the night of the murder. Much of what I will tell you now is simply conjecture, so I might be wrong on some of the details, but this is how you did it.

"You ran out of the house, pretending to chase after Kōjin, and carried the plastic bags with the body parts to the back door. You were careful to avoid being noticed by Kuramoto as you snuck back inside the house and made your way to Kiichi's rooms. Yurie was probably still there. You went over to Kiichi, pretending to report to him on your chase, but the moment you saw an opportunity, you struck him on the head with a blunt instrument. He immediately fell out of his wheelchair, sprawling across the floor. You did this not in the sitting room, but in the room next door: the study. Then you carried Kiichi's body to the secret basement room via the study—"

"No." I finally couldn't contain myself any longer. "Shimada... Wait, what am I doing? I don't have to put on this fake voice any more." I dropped the hoarse rasp and carried on speaking naturally. "I won't pretend any more. You've got most of it right. Except for that last bit."

"What do you mean?"

"I didn't know about the secret room in the study. I suspected there was such a room somewhere in this house, since it was built by Nakamura Seiji, and I guessed it would be in the study, but I never managed to find it. When you mentioned the name Nakamura Seiji to me yesterday and hinted at some connection with him, it got my hopes up that I might finally be able to locate it. That's why I decided to invite you into the house."

"You didn't know about the secret room?" Shimada blinked a few times, but then gave a satisfied nod.

"Aha, that's why it all looked so careless! Could you explain the rest to us, Masaki?"

After carrying the eight bags containing Furukawa's body parts, his clothes and the tools I used to cut him up to the back door, I snuck back into the house. First I looked inside the stairwell room to check on the supposedly stolen painting, then I went straight to Kiichi's rooms. Yurie was sitting on the sofa in the sitting room, while he was in the study.

I hid the spanner I had brought with me behind my back and entered the study. Kiichi didn't suspect a thing. He was sitting at his desk, listening to my made-up account when I struck him on the head with all my might. I could feel the dark flames of revenge burning inside me as I hit my friend, the person responsible for the accident twelve years before.

He fell off his wheelchair, collapsing on the carpet. A weak groan escaped his lips, but eventually he stopped moving.

Yurie had come to the study to check on me at that very moment, but the horrifying scene playing out in front of her gave her a terrible shock. She had a dizzy spell and fainted on the floor.

Startled, I left the corpse of Fujinuma Kiichi (or so I thought) lying there and immediately went to help her up. She was trembling all over, so I tried to calm her down while I walked her back to the tower room and got her into bed.

I then hurried back to Kiichi's quarters. It was on the way that I heard Kuramoto's voice.

He had apparently stumbled upon the painting on the stairwell landing. (I had foolishly neglected to close the door completely when I'd had a look at the painting earlier.) I waited for him in the hallway and used an ornament sitting nearby to knock him out. I brought heavy string from the store cupboard and tied him up. I used Furukawa's handkerchief as a gag and moved Kuramoto into a corner of the dining room. I had been carrying the handkerchief around with me, with the intention of dropping it somewhere outside the house.

I ran back to Kiichi's quarters. I still had work to do. My plan was to wait and eventually bury his body somewhere in the woods.

But he had vanished from the study!

I panicked. There were faint bloodstains on the carpet. I thought Kiichi was dead when he fell from his wheelchair after I had hit him and he stopped moving, but was he still alive? His

244

wheelchair was still here. He couldn't have gone far without it and with such a bad injury to his head.

I looked in the bedroom and outside in the gallery, but he was nowhere to be found. The others in the house were astounded by Furukawa's vanishing from the first-floor annex, but to me it was Fujinuma Kiichi's disappearance that was inexplicable!

After some serious thought, I arrived at a conclusion.

There had to be a hidden passage somewhere in the study, and he had managed to flee to a secret room only he knew of. I knew about Nakamura Seiji's work, and Kiichi himself had once hinted at the existence of a secret room somewhere, in which Issei's final work *The Phantom Cluster* was kept, hidden from the world.

I began looking for the entrance to the room.

Badly injured and without his wheelchair, Kiichi could not have gone far. The entrance had to be somewhere inside the study. But I was in shock at this sudden turn of events and still had a lot of work ahead of me. I couldn't look for it just then.

Afterwards I searched the study again and again, but never managed to find a hidden passage or the secret room. I eventually grew to fear the vanished man's ghost and decided to keep the study sealed.

That is why I was so interested in the unsolved aspects of the case. I was terrified of the man who had disappeared under impossible circumstances, of his ghost that roamed the house. While I strongly suspected that Yurie was the author of the threatening note and the person who had unlocked the door to the study, I could never truly escape my fear that the missing man had returned.

*

Shimada Kiyoshi nodded.

"Aha, I mistakenly assumed it was you who hid the body down there."

"Where was it? How did you manage to get into the secret room?" I asked.

"It was just luck, to be honest," said Shimada modestly, running his hand through his dust-caked hair.

"I was convinced there was some secret hidden inside this study when I heard the room was never opened. I suspected there was a hidden passage leading to a secret room. My instinct told me that it was likely going to be a basement room, and that there'd need to be a lift to go down there. Remember that Kuramoto heard a strange creaking sound on the night of the murder? Considering the time at which he had heard the noise, I suspected that was the sound of the lift in operation.

"If my hunch was correct, and if *The Phantom Cluster* was also stored in the secret room, I realized that the painting had been moved into the room somehow, and it was too big to fit in the lift—so there had to be at least one other entrance to the room somewhere. Such an entrance would also be necessary for repairs if the lift broke down. I also figured that the mill wheels, the 'symbol' of this house, would probably play an important role. Anyway, that was all just speculation.

"I confided part of my thoughts to Kuramoto, and had a look inside the turbine room."

"The turbine room? Did you find anything there?"

"Yes. All the way at the back, there's a line in the floor. It's practically invisible unless you are looking for it. I searched the floor and found something like a handle hidden behind one of the machines. It was a trap door. And as I had expected, there were stairs below it.

"There was also a light switch, so I immediately went down. And I found a large basement room, right beneath the turbine room, extending out in the direction of the Western Gallery. And there it was, hanging on the wall. The painting all of you want to see so dearly."

"*The Phantom Cluster*?"

"It's there!?" Ōishi and Mori cried out simultaneously.

"Did you find it?"

"Did you really see it?"

"Yes, with my own two eyes." Shimada frowned. "And I think I understand why Kiichi didn't want anyone else to see that painting. Masaki, I assume you haven't seen the painting yourself then?"

I shook my head. Shimada's frown deepened.

"Oh, well, forget it."

Shimada then went back to his explanation.

"A corpse was lying on its stomach on the floor, its hand reaching out towards the painting. It was Fujinuma Kiichi. I had of course suspected I'd find him there, but I have to admit I was scared out of my wits at the sight."

"... How did you get up into the study?"

"There is a small lift cage behind his remains. It was just large enough to hold a man sitting in a wheelchair. I entered the cage and pushed the black switch on the control panel in the back of the cage. And with a fair amount of noise the cage slowly went up. All the way up, into the fireplace in the study."

"The fireplace…"

"The firebox itself is the cage of the lift. I think there's an open space behind the flue and the wall which holds the motor. There are probably two fireboxes, exactly the same size, one right above the other. You ride the lower box, and as it goes down into the

247

secret basement room, the upper firebox descends to take its place inside the fireplace. I assume you couldn't find anything when you looked because the control panel is only built into the lower firebox.

"That was the mystery behind the secret room, and as for the rest of the crime. I don't think I need to explain any more, do I?

"You carried the plastic bags you had left near the back door to the basement. You used the incinerator to burn the body parts as well as Kōjin's clothes and the tools you used. You also burned the clothes you, Masaki Shingo, had been wearing. You had already cut off Kōjin's left finger when you were cutting up the body. You probably got rid of it later, by burying it in the woods or something like that.

"Next came the most dreadful part of your plan. You had to cut off your own left ring finger. Did you use the heated poker to cauterize the wound? I can't imagine how horrible it must have been. I wouldn't have been able to do it, even if I had painkillers ready.

"You removed your ring and dropped your finger on the basement floor, ready for the others to find. Did you keep your ring, or throw it in the river? In any case, you yourself dressed in Kiichi's clothes, stuffing the ring finger of his left glove, and put on one of his masks. After taking on the persona of the master of the house, you waited for the body to burn for a while before you went out and helped free Kuramoto. Yurie added another lie about having seen Furukawa from the tower room window, after which you attracted Kuramoto's attention to the smoke coming out of the chimney. And that's how you ended up 'discovering' the body. I suspect that the so-called stolen painting is hidden somewhere among the many other paintings kept in the archive.

"And so by 'killing' Masaki Shingo and framing Furukawa Kōjin as the culprit, you were reborn as Fujinuma Kiichi. The thirty-eight years of your previous life had been reduced to dust. In return you were freed from the talons of justice descending on you for the crime you had committed in Tōkyō, and gained an immense fortune as well as the woman you loved."

Shimada stopped and took a deep breath.

He looked at his wristwatch and then took out the small cigarette case from the pocket of his jeans. He put his one cigarette of the day between his lips. He seemed as if he were looking for the right words to conclude his speech, like the great detectives of yore.

At that moment, the sound of the never-ending rain and the rumble of the mill wheels outside were joined by a cacophony of wailing sirens. The police had arrived.

FUJINUMA KIICHI'S BEDROOM ~ STUDY ~ SECRET ROOM (4:50 A.M.)

While everyone was distracted by the sound of the approaching sirens. I took the opportunity to jump up from the wheelchair, shove Shimada's lanky figure out of my way and dart straight for the bedroom.

Ignoring the yells from behind as I ran into the bedroom, I closed the door behind me and locked it immediately.

"Masaki, open the door! Let us in!"

Shimada was yelling desperately. He kept banging on the door.

Yurie was sitting on the bed. She had the duvet wrapped around her and looked terrified.

"You heard him, right?" I asked. I took off the white rubber mask that had been my face for a year. It dropped to the floor.

"Yurie. Do you still love me?"

I finally managed to ask her the question directly. She cocked her head slightly. Her eyes were wide open, staring at my real face.

"I—I don't know."

She spoke those words clearly. The summer before last, when I played the piano for her in the tower room, she had whispered words of love back to me. (Now I was missing a finger on my left hand, I wasn't able to play the piano for her like I had back then.) Those same lips had now spoken differently, of her own will.

She had been held captive in this house for over a decade. It was I, Masaki Shingo, who had first managed to show her the world, the "outside". She learned what it was to love, what it was to be loved by a man. And by listening to him and helping him, her pure hands became stained by a bloody crime. And when she again found herself trapped in the peaceful world that man had longed for, she again found herself longing for the world outside.

At that moment I finally realized: Yurie wasn't a doll simply obeying my orders any more.

I had loved that beautiful doll who'd been deprived of her spirit by Fujinuma Kiichi, and I had given her life. The doll had gained a will of her own, and now she was about to walk off and leave me.

Perhaps it was just the stupid sentimentality of a fallen criminal, but somehow I could accept that. I do accept it.

I was in a curious state of mind. The burning flames I felt when I killed Mitamura were calm as the sea now.

I knew I'd be caught and pay the highest price as a ruthless murderer. But I still wanted to save her somehow. I had to carry the burden of these crimes alone.

"I'm sorry. I hope you will be able to forgive me," I said, then turned around and ran into the study. I could hear Shimada and the others crying for me from the other side of the wall.

"Don't worry. I won't do anything foolish. I only want to have a look at the painting," I cried as I slipped into the fireplace.

As Shimada had explained, there was a small black switch hidden in the back of the firebox. I pushed it gently and there it was: the creaking sound I had heard before.

The cage descended slowly and then arrived at its destination. The secret basement room. At that exact moment, I covered my mouth and gave a weak, frightened cry.

He was lying right in front of me, underneath the light shining down from the low ceiling: Fujinuma Kiichi.

A whole year had passed, but for some reason his body hadn't fully decomposed to a skeleton yet. Or was it my imagination? Dried bits of flesh were still visible on the exposed bones. Was I imagining that too? His mask had discoloured. His dressing gown was caked in dust. An awful smell hung in the air around him…

I remembered that Nozawa Tomoko had complained about an unpleasant smell in the basement. This secret room must be next door to it. The smell would have penetrated through minuscule slits and cracks in the wall to the other side.

Kiichi's white-gloved right hand was stretched out in front of his body. My eyes followed the direction it indicated, until they came to a large canvas hanging on the wall.

The Phantom Cluster!

I covered my mouth. My mouth fell open in astonishment. I looked up at the uncanny painting before me, forgetting all about the pungent smell.

A gigantic dark silhouette filled the whole canvas. It was a European-style castle with a tower. And to the left of that outline, three wheels. Mill wheels? Yes, they were mill wheels.

It was this house. It was the Mill House. And inside the house, a series of strange images were drawn.

The first was a beautiful woman with long black hair. She had a sad look in her large eyes, which seemed to stare far off into the distance.

The second was a pair of pale legs, straight as tree trunks.

And what was that floating at the centre of the house? It was a mask. A creepy white mask, like that which covered the face of Issei's own son, Fujinuma Kiichi.

"'I'm just as afraid of that painting as my father was. You could even say I detest it.'"

I then recalled what Kiichi had told me about the painting: that his father was capable of seeing fantastical visions.

So that was what he meant. Issei's imagination had been the inspiration for all those fantastical landscapes, but not in the way we all assumed. People called him a visionary artist, but the truth was he had literally seen visions: he had been suffering from hallucinations. Issei was a prodigy, a seer, who painted the fantastical visions he saw with his mind's eye.

How shocked Kiichi must have been thirteen years ago, when he lost the use of his legs in that accident. His father Issei had predicted his son's future in this painting.

I looked at the canvas in awe.

Kiichi dreaded the ominous future his father had predicted. And yet he'd been guided by it, deciding to build a house with three mill wheels.

Everything had happened because of this painting.

It was because of this painting that his house had to be the Mill House. It was because of this painting that this house had become one of the strange creations of the crazed architect Nakamura Seiji. It was because of this painting that Kiichi had decided to wear a mask and retreat into this house with the black-haired beauty Yurie. And that's why he kept the painting hidden away…

At that moment, my eye fell on something small painted in a corner of *The Phantom Cluster*. I couldn't hold back the cry that escaped from my throat.

No, how could it be!?

Was I a victim of the same fate as Kiichi?

It was a hand, held palm out towards the viewer, its fingers stiffly spread. It was all there in the painting: a left hand, covered in grey blood, missing the second finger from the right.